HER LEGEND LIVES IN YOU

THE UNTOLD CREATION STORY HONORING THE GODDESS AND OUR DAUGHTERS

AS DISCOVERED BY M.J.C.

PUBLISHING

Published by Dear Dean Publishing
Sacramento, CA.

22 Goddess Symbols created by Myron J. Clifton and Katya J. Lerner. Design by Katya J. Lerner / Buzzword Consulting.

Layout and cover design by Lisa Ham
(Cover firefly photo: wplynn/flickr)

PREFACE

The winter of 1964 found me on vacation in New Zealand, watching the local All Blacks rugby team perform a Haka of death, in an acknowledgment of the recent death of a beloved rugby player. The Haka — often done as a challenge or war chant, is an emotional performance by the Maori, the local indigenous people of New Zealand. Later, when speaking with local friends of my host, they answered my inquiry with a clear accounting of the Haka we had all just witnessed. It was the Haka of *Papa* or, in the Maori language — **Mother Earth.**

In 1971 while visiting a certain Polynesian island, I recalled to a culture center guide my Haka story of Papa — Mother Earth. She smiled politely and said, "Yes. And do you know of Hina, she of Mother Earth?" She directed me to the "Old Ones," in Australia. The Aboriginal peoples of Australia have been found to have occupied Australia for 70–100,000 years, representing the first migration out of Africa.

In Southeast Australia I listened to an Elder slowly recount the story of "Birra-ngulu," Daughter of the Goddess. When I asked a simple follow-up question the Elder simply said: "You know not of the Daughter." He stated it as a fact, and he was correct.

Thus began my obsession to discover the hidden Goddess, Mother, and Daughter.

Subsequent visits took me in 1979 to Egypt, China, and Iran, 1981 to Iraq, Israel, and Ethiopia, 1988 to Oman, 1989 to Honduras and El Salvador, 1993 to Italy, Germany, and Russia, and to many other places where I learned the many names of a Goddess who seemed to be versions of a single entity. I also started to piece together that perhaps this unnamed Goddess/Mother had a Daughter.

Their names varied, of course, but the stories told were remarkably similar and, most unique, all of the people who spoke of either the Goddess/Mother or the Daughter acknowledged their own limited understanding and asked that I seek out others for their interpretation. This was surprising considering how all beliefs today are predicated upon absolutism of believers. The names of the Goddess/Mother/Daughter that were shared were historical: Inanna, Nut, Isis, Astarte, Ariniti, Uzza, Prithvi, Gaia, Freyja, Kali, Coatlicue, Pachamama, Ixchel, Amaterasu, Valentina, Devi, Ruach.

And, finally, in Sudan, the Southern Nuba people confidently and clearly told me of the Goddess, who they call "Great Mother," and she who gave birth to all things and to humans.

I completed my work of recording, translating, and organizing the stories into this book. As I learned from each of the cultures, this is an incomplete telling, and there are certain inaccuracies that are accepted within the cultures.

What is agreed upon by all groups is: The Goddess, sometimes called the Mother, and her Daughter are real, alive, and are creators of all things.

~M.J.C. November 29, 2017

WISDOM

RELIGION

BIRTHING

FRIENDS

CREATION

MOTHERS

STRUCTURE

PROCESS

LOVE

BEGINNING

GARDEN

RELIGION

All of religion is merely men mansplaining God.

The Goddess laughed to herself. She created all things, but not in her image, no, she longed for difference and diversity. She was a curious creator who did not know the reach of her powers.

She was favored by the Original. The Original was the true God and Creator. And the Original God was everywhere and most often in the form of what the Goddess and other Gods simply called: Wind.

In her existence she explored large places and small, all pasts and all futures. She saw Gods rise and fade – Gods never "died" in the sense of how what they created died. Gods faded back to the Original to start over.

There were old Gods she remembered and missed; she could still reach them, feel them, and even share time with them, but in their faded state she could not commune too long lest she also start to fade.

She was young by God standards. Just over twenty-two billion years.

She didn't want to separate from the Original; no God did. But in this one way, and only one way, did the Gods not have a choice. The Original said it must happen.

And so it happened.

After these years as part of the Original, it was time for her to leave; her Great Separation was come.

She paused when she first realized it was her time, and in that pause two billion years passed.

Then she felt the Great Separation happening and she experienced sadness for the first time. And she knew love on another level. And she knew so much more.

She better understood the Original now and why the Great Separation was.

The Original shared with her over a brief million years while considering her. Then there was silence for a few million more years as the Original created her name.

Her time was now and it had all happened so fast.

Then the Original made sound of the wind that she would forever pause to hear, listen to, and respond to. It was the sound of love, of longing, of wanting, and of unyielding expectation. It was the sound of life, and of passion, and of joy beyond measure. It was the Original and it was the Goddess. It was the word of all things past and future.

And the word filled the Goddess fully with knowledge of all things and most importantly the word filled the Goddess with purpose.

And then she did what all Gods did in this moment: She created. She created unlike any God before or since.

She was the Goddess.

And the Goddess spoke and said: *Let there be light!*

And into nothingness she created a new Universe.

And at that same instant when she created all things she said her name at last and infused all of her Creation with her name.

A single eternal name that spread through the Goddess to all of her Creation:

Mother.

BIRTHING

All of Creation is merely a birthing story.

The echo of her first birth can still be heard in all the Universe. The sound is in the background of all universal sounds.

The Goddess was busy!

With her name singing an eternal song during those first few nano-seconds, the Goddess opened herself and her power flowed all at once and in all directions in a magnificent expression of herself.

And in those milliseconds her Universe was now immeasurable.

This was the first birth in her new Universe. The Goddess' power was soft, curved, slow and smooth. There were a few sharp angles but she preferred gentle bends, segues, and agreement in form and all that she created.

The Original's name for the Goddess informed her purpose, and her essence fueled her creative expressions.

In those first few million years the Goddess played with things that would forever be unseen but which would be studied and she left her presence in all things she birthed.

All things in her Universe are made of her.

The Goddess paused to observe her Universe and then she smiled to herself.

She knew what her Universe needed. *I will make a garden,* the Goddess said.

What is purpose if not growing and tending a garden where one may con-template, she asked and answered herself.

And so, she planted simple galaxies and spiral galaxies, there and there. *Just a simple garden,* she told herself.

Next were gas clouds that were as big as galaxies, and nebulas that were as original in all universes as they were awe-inspiring. She grew stars that burned slowly — *perennials* she called them, and others that burned out quickly in a few billion years — *seasonals,* those were called.

She planted black holes, strung star systems all around, and placed comets and asteroid belts all over.

And she took from her own light and planted growing balls of fire to warm her garden while night stars and moons kept her garden comforted, and to provide for the small things that she planted in the garden — to live, feed, and help the garden birth its own.

Finally, over there she decided to plant orbs that circled her stars and to the orbs some were given their own orbs that circled them. And they were given fire to help forge the garden.

The Goddess paused for a few billion years before noticing one of her stars calling to her because it was lonely.

Then she smiled a mischievous smile and laughed to herself at her garden — it was lovely!

She was well pleased but not finished!

The star that called to her informed her that one of the orbs was sad and longed for the Goddess' attention.

And she heard her orb and attended to it, listened to it, and answered it.

And the Goddess gave the orb purpose.

To the lonely star — all of them — the Goddess gave them purpose as well, for that is what all things desire.

In totality their purpose was intertwined forever and it was art. And they had uniqueness as did all of her Creation.

And so the Goddess established her benevolence in her Universe.

And in those next moments, those few billion years, her universal garden began birthing its art in a joyous and never-ending attempt to win her favor and her attention.

There was wave after wave of color, form, intent, mystery, laughter, love, longing, sadness, and even anger. The angry art was dreadful in its power. The loving art was dreadful in its power. The art would be called: Day. Night. Sun. Sky. Fire. Mountain. Volcano. Space. Darkness. Abstract. Unknown. It was called power. And loss. And mystery.

And it was called glory. But mostly it was called art.

Billions of years passed and one of the orbs she planted was struggling. Every time it tried to show the Goddess art that expressed her essence, this orb felt unsatisfied.

She gave the orb the first gift in her universe: Hope.

The orb welcomed the Goddess' favor! The orb had purpose and hope now.

Hope. Always hope.

The orb quickly began working on its own garden over the next few billion years.

The orb turned this way and that, and it summoned color from deep inside itself; it took gifts from other orbs and mixed the ingredients to birth new art materials; it was pleased, but not finished. Small things grew large and in those things the orb shared its purpose. All things on the orb now worked in unison to express themselves in a garden of art to please their Goddess.

The Goddess had watched this orb in these early billion years and she was pleased and curious at how hard the orb had worked for her. Her attention to the orb added color, and her joy at the art the orb was creating produced water on the orb. They were the Goddess' tears of love and joy.

The orb called these tears water. Or rain. Or life. Or ocean. Or river. Or stream. Or lake. Or waterfall. Or storm. Or liquid. Or waves. The orb couldn't settle on one word so all were used.

Those tears immediately brought new art to the orb, for her tears contained her colors.

Color!

Just a few hundred-thousand colors at first. And then millions. Then trillions.

All around the orb was color. All possible colors.

And the Goddess was pleased with her garden. She loved all her gardens in her Universe and all were pleasing to her and all found her favor.

All received her essence and her color.

And the Goddess decided to rest in her garden on this now blue orb.

Receiving her favor, the blue orb and all its color, oceans, mountains, and volcanoes shouted to the Goddess in unison:

Our Mother is welcome!

As the Goddess and Mother rested in her garden, her essence fed the orb in all its oceans, fields, sky, mountains, and forests.

And the blue orb, feeding off the Goddess' essence all these billions of years finally settled down.

But the Goddess' essence stayed busy these next few billion years and her blue orb and garden became part of her. And she returned their love.

And the Goddess was now Mother Earth, as she was always meant to be.

FRIENDS

Creation is merely an expression of wanting friends.

As the Goddess rested, eons passed and her garden bloomed all over the orb with colors that reflected the Mother's joy and love for her creation.

Resting for the Goddess did not mean rest from creating. During her rest, the Goddess focused on all the small details that creating and art required.

She explored her orb and as she did so she created valleys, and caves, and waterfalls, and deserts and rivers, and hills, and rocks, and cliffs, and islands and gulfs and ditches.

And she decided to rearrange some landmasses to better suit her designer's eye. She wanted everything in its place.

She was preparing the water, sky, and land.

She decided that her little blue orb and her garden needed protection from some of her other creations that now traveled the universe riding the wind. So she placed a protective aura around its circumference, and she settled her waters by placing the Moon in just the right place.

There. That was better.

And now the landmasses were in place and the waters flowed everywhere.

She was joyous, and a joyous Goddess is the light of all Creation — and thus, all of Creation rejoiced with her in all times past, present, and future. And all the old and new Gods and the Original marveled at the Goddess and her Universe. And the Universe sang the Goddess' song from old without ceasing even until now.

The Goddess continued to rest and to create. And she dreamed. For in her dreams resided special things she'd waited twenty-two billion years to share.

Her special things included flowers — flowers that captured her colors. She asked them to spread throughout her orb, in her waters, on her mountains, and in all valleys and deserts.

Trees were next. She asked them to keep watch over all lands, to tell the sky when the orb needed water, or heat, or wind, or fire, and to tell the orb when the sky was going to send water, or heat, or wind, or fire. She also told the trees and flowers that she'd soon give them friends.

The flowers and trees danced in love at their Goddess and they spread throughout her garden in joy as she intended.

The Goddess smiled and continued to rest.

The Goddess so loved her world that she gave of herself so that all her creation could also create their own kind.

Millions of years later the friends of the flowers and trees had done their job and now the garden was full. Then the Goddess communed with her Matter: atoms, cells, bacteria, germs —. These were some of her smallest creations, and she imparted love to them and asked that they stay busy; for theirs was the unseen work that guided all things, and their importance would not always be seen but she would be with them always to love them, play with them, and show them joy and laughter.

The Goddess rested.

And while she rested she explored her oceans and she communed there for a few million years and when she finally moved on little things were swimming around in her oceans.

The Goddess visited streams near her oceans and when she left she bade the little things that were swimming around to follow her to the land. And so they did.

They followed her for the next few hundred million years as she toured her garden with and for them. And the creatures now walked, or ran, or climbed, and when she wanted to show them the sky, some started flying for they did not want their Goddess to go on without them!

The Goddess rested.

And even as she did, she was aware of a disturbance near her. Then another. The Goddess rested still, though she was aware of these two disturbances near her.

They watched her rest. The resting Goddess considered them.

They were small gods. Small creatures who told her they loved her and wanted to be with her always.

One, she summoned closer. It bounded to her, happy, and with a loud noise that caused the Goddess to laugh. It jumped into her arms and licked her and then, jumping down, spun round and round sang a song of harsh yet happy sounds and its sound tickled the Goddess and its movement brought her joy. The little tail was moving and the creature started licking the Goddess again trying to love her. She loved it back and it was settled.

You will be my companion, beast. Come to your Goddess and love me; I will love you back, Dog.

And the dog-god did as she was told and she was pleased to finally be with her Goddess. And the Goddess blessed her, then said: Dog, please go and eternally search for the answer to this question: *Who's a good dog?* And the dog ran away to find the answer.

The Goddess turned her attention to the other god. She was smaller still and patiently watching the Goddess and the other creature, now called Dog.

The little creature did not move. She studied her surroundings and that was it.

The Goddess studied her back. Their eyes met. Ten million years later the little creature quietly said: You are my Goddess. Even though you only met my eyes for ten million years, and that's not quite long enough, it is perhaps the best you can do, my Goddess, so I accept you.

The Goddess didn't move. She continued to look the little creature in the eyes, unblinking. And now, finally, fifteen million more years passed and then the Goddess spoke:

Come to me, my familiar, I am your Goddess.

Five million years later the creature started walking to her Goddess.

A million years later, having finally arrived to the Goddess, the creature wrapped herself around her Goddess and said *Meow,* so loudly that the universe shook, and then the little creature started purring and mountains crumbled and giant waves crashed the lands forming little hiding places for future creatures such as this one.

Then the creature jumped into her Goddess' arms and said quietly: You are my Goddess. I will stay.

And the Goddess said back: You are my familiar, Cat, I will allow you to stay.

⁓ 24 ⁓

And the cat went to sleep in her Goddess' arms and the dog set about making canyons all across the blue orb.

The Goddess rested.

CREATION

Creation is merely multitasking on a universal scale.

The Goddess rested on her blue orb and she also tended to her Universe. The Goddess was, after all, in all places and in all times in her Universe and so she tended to her Universe, which really was her playground.

Understanding what was to come, the Goddess established rules and guidelines for her Universe. She also hid secrets that would slowly be found in sequences that she decided.

The Goddess created many rules, such as gravity, speed limits, decay, inertia, thermodynamics, motion, force, quantum physics, absolute zero, attraction and space time. There are many more that will take billions of years to discover, the Goddess decided.

The Universe celebrated the Goddess and rejoiced in her rules and guidelines.

The Goddess knew the curious would seek answers in her heavens and so she sprinkled secrets here and there, placed anomalies where they'd be hidden, but not hidden too much because she knew discovery would be a purpose and it would be celebrated. She left clues that wanted to be found and she left clues that did not want to be found, but would be found, but that would not give up their secrets. She giggled at her secrets and clues because of the story they told about all things.

And she left her Echo, her Strings, and her Aura as evidence of her presence, and it stretched throughout her universe as proof of the first birth.

The Goddess was pleased and still multitasking. For, while she established rules and guidelines for her universe, she also did the same on her blue orb.

On the blue orb she asked the cat to hide magic all across the orb, but in the cat's hidden places. And the cat rejoiced, finally, because she liked hiding things. So she set about hiding magic all over the orb, in trees, valleys, caves, near streams, under rocks, in flower fields, and in a few places that would allow just enough magic to be found, but not enough to cause a magic-rush. And she shared magic with some other creatures including crows, owls, robins, bluebirds, peacocks, fowls, osprey, hawks, eagles, ducks, and especially penguins because the cat-god didn't quite know what the Goddess was thinking when she created penguins.

The cat-god also gave magic to the dragon. And the dragon immediately set out to use her magic to take magic from other magical beings and hide her magic and other things in giant mountains that she forged with fire from her mouth. This didn't bother the cat, though, because the cat could even control the dragon. But other creatures were afraid of the dragon, so the Goddess stopped by the dragon's mountain, kissed the dragon and told her how beautiful she was, and promised her that while she may keep her magic, she was simply too big and all the other creatures were afraid of her.

The dragon understood the Goddess and asked for just these favors: Please allow me still to fly, my Goddess, and please let me keep my holy fire.

The Goddess considered the dragon's request, and because she loved the dragon — the dragon was also her child — she agreed to honor the dragon's desires.

So the Goddess split the dragon in two and made both new dragons much smaller. One of the now-smaller dragons was called a firefly, for she kept her holy fire, and the other was now called a dragonfly, and she kept the beauty of the dragon's colorful armor. Both could still fly, as promised, and one held the holy fire that would no longer be able to forge mountain caves but would burn brightly in the night, lighting the way for other creatures. And the dragonfly would populate her gardens with their wonderful colors that matched the many flowers.

And of course, the cat kept a lot of magic for herself and shared none with the dog.

The Goddess laughed at the cat-god and the dog-god for she knew these gods had been going on like this forever and forever. She loved them. And so the Goddess made sure that the dog was always able to find magic with her nose as long as it was wet.

The Goddess then brought rules and guidelines to the orb. She filled the orb with logic, and magnetism, numbers, cause and effect, healing, forgiveness, Yin and Yang, Karma, The Golden Rule, knowledge, gardening, chocolate, Zen, seasons, fun, sprinkles, snow, and twenty-two senses (six to start, twenty-two total).

She gave magic to the Moon and asked that it gradually release a little magic once a month and the Moon laughed and laughed. Then she turned to the Sun and shone her countenance on the Sun and the Sun understood what it was to do. The Sun moved just a bit and then fully illuminated for the first time, and brightness and warmth, healing and happiness covered the orb.

The Goddess then whispered to the orb, and in her whisper were humor and laughing, jokes and funny stories and endless giggles.

Then, finally, the Goddess added tears of joy and of pain, sorrow, and loss, and beginnings and endings.

When the endings were established, the Goddess cried for all her Creation. And Creation cried too but not out of self-pity; Creation cried because the Goddess cried, for her sorrow was unbearable and the Universe wanted its own ending to end the sorrow.

This time was forever known as The Great Sadness. All future sadness would have its origin in this moment.

All Gods stopped in reverence and cried for the Goddess, for her sorrow was the sorrow of all Creation in all universes and in all pasts and all futures.

No universe was ever the same, and from that moment of the Great Sadness until the No-End of Time, all universes held a place of reverential sorrow for the Goddess.

Even the Wind was still across all universes.

After many eons, the Great Sadness ended for the Goddess. And she paused to reflect on her young Creation, which was just over fourteen billion years old. Her garden was thriving and the creatures she'd led out of the waters were now spread all across the land, the seas, the air, and deserts, forests, plains, caves, mountains, fields, shores, and all points in between.

With the rules and guidelines in place and the garden ready, the Goddess knew the time was ripe for the orb to give birth.

So the Goddess sent the rain.

MOTHERS

All births are from mothers.

The Goddess' rain covered the orb fully. The oceans were the highest ever and some flooded lands so much that in the future stories would be told of a Great Flood. The rain continued. Many trees were underwater and many mountains now looked like hills. Creatures who lived in some areas now had to move elsewhere, and other creatures moved to other places.

The Goddess' rain continued for many years so that all areas of the blue orb garden were now soaked.

The cat-god had easily found a place to ignore the rain and sleep. She looked up occasionally to see what all the fuss was about, but mostly she was unbothered and continued her sleep. The dog-god thought the rain was the perfect time to play in the mud. So she did. She played all over the blue orb, splashing about and generally making a gigantic mess of things, and waylaid her from her search for the answer to the question the Goddess set her out to answer: *Who's a good dog?*

Finally, after thousands of years, the Goddess stopped the rain. She thanked the clouds and scattered them so that the Goddess' rain would never again come in such volume. And she took colors from some of her garden flowers and spread them across the sky, in a beautiful curve that recalled some of the colors in other parts of her Universe that she wanted to share with the orb. She said the universal colors in the sky would always be a reminder that there are sky colors in the Universe.

Then she was again Mother, and she entered her orb in all places at once and felt all her creatures, all her water, all her plants and trees, and atoms, and rocks, and minerals, and bacteria. She felt all the air, and it contained tiny parts of her Universe that had traveled to the orb to be part of the First Great Birth.

And then the Goddess summoned all parts of her orb to her: *Come to your Goddess; Come to your Mother.* And they all came to their Goddess and Mother.

And the orb slowly started shaking as all parts of it, and all of its visitors, moved to the Mother. The Mother received them all in celebration and joy, in familiar greeting, and in homecoming. Though all parts of the blue orb communed with the Mother at all times, others from the Universe did not — though they communed with the Goddess. And there was happy recognition, and old friends crying tears of joy as they all gathered to the Mother.

And the Mother welcomed them all.

And still they came. Millions. Billions. Trillions. And then more. All to the Mother for the First Birth.

All of the heavens paused. All other universes and their Gods paused and were silent, and the Wind was again still. The cat-god waited patiently while the dog-god sat at attention wagging a tail that was clearing space the size of a continent.

It happened quickly, in just over 6,220,000 years, when out of the Mother, She came.

The silence was broken as the First Birth happened. All of existence wanted to know. All Gods waited for they also wanted to know. (This was the first time the other Gods did not know something, and thus they waited with the rest of all of Creation and the Wind.)

The Mother Goddess broke the silence with a smile, and then a tear. And then holy tears of joy permeated all universes all at once. The power of her joy and her holy tears changed time and space, changed orbits and calculations, changed Matter and dark matter, changed all pasts and all futures.

The Mother Goddess' holy tears of joy forever and forever changed all Gods in all universes and again caused the Wind to still. And then the Wind did something that it had never done before and never will do again: The Wind honored the Mother Goddess as God. *She has come. She has taken her place that was to be. She Is. She is Always. She is the Mother Goddess.*

And then the holy tears caused the Sun to increase and the Moon to glow, and on the orb, which was now the Orb, trees grew higher and creatures bigger, faster, and stronger; small elements expanded their presence and birds translated the joy into song. And large elements moved this way and that.

The cat-god looked on. The dog-god barked and caused rivers to change course.

And then the Mother Goddess, summoning all her pasts and futures named her First Great Birth, who was tethered to the Mother and the Orb, with her eyes open and her tiny and chubby hands trying to grab something, anything, and her fat feet true perfection, and her cheeks ready to be smooshed. Her head was bald like the Moon and the Moon was happy about that! Her eyes sparkled like the Stars and the Stars celebrated the First Great Birth. The Sun, who never thought to witness something brighter than itself, other than the Goddess, of course, saw pure light in the First Born's mouth which formed a curve like that which the Goddess left in the sky following the Goddess' rain. The Sun celebrated with bursts and streams of Sun fire that burned like this every time the Sun recalled this day — these were later called sunflares.

Then the Mother spoke: Come to me, Daughter; I am your Mother Goddess.

And the Daughter answered with a sound that would forever echo in all time; in a new language that only the Mother Goddess understood. A sound that made the cat-god's eyes open wider and then caused her to seek shelter; a sound that caused the dog-god to howl in happiness or pain; and a sound that parted clouds, caused the birds to fly, and the oceans to return to their former boundaries.

The Mother Goddess smiled as her Daughter cried.

Then the Mother Goddess took the form of her Daughter and everything changed.

STRUCTURE

The Universe and children love structure.

Much happened during the early few hundred thousand years with the Goddess and her Daughter. There are many stories and adventures that happened with and between them. And the Orb never stopped birthing other daughters as well. But the end of their story has not and will not ever come, for they will always be Mother and Daughter — Goddess and her First Birth. First of the Orb, and First in the Universe.

The glorious titles soon met the pleasure of raising the First Daughter.

The Goddess called her Daughter to her and said: *Now you will sleep.* And the Daughter replied: *But I don't want to sleep, Mother; you never sleep, so I don't have to either.* And at that, the Daughter started running as fast as she could. She couldn't outrun the Mother, of course, for the Mother was everywhere at once. But the Daughter didn't know that, yet, and so the Mother chased her over hills, into and out of four or five oceans, up trees, and into caves and hiding places. The dog-god ran with the Daughter.

These chases usually only lasted a few thousand years and of course the Mother never tired, and for that matter neither did the Daughter nor the dog-god. A few times the Mother just let her run herself to sleep, and on those occasions it was usually the cat-god who brought her back. The dog-god never brought her back because she never tired, either. She shared with the Daughter her quest to find the answer to the eternal question: *Who's a good dog?* And the Daughter was determined to help discover the answer.

Often the Mother would sing her Daughter to sleep. One time, when the Mother sang the Daughter's favorite sleep song:

Good night, little Daughter, good night

Good night, little Daughter, good night

Are you sleeping or are you playing?

Good night little Daughter, good night (repeat four or five hundred thousand times)

all the creatures slept, and the Orb was quiet and the waters still. The Mother's singing rang throughout the Universe and all her Creation felt safe, warm, loved, and cozy.

The Mother sang for hundreds of years and all of Creation felt the fullness of the Goddess's love.

Finally, when the Mother knew the Daughter had finally gone to sleep she stopped singing and looked down at her Daughter.

The Daughter's beautiful eyes looked back at the Mother. She was wide awake.

Daughter, why aren't you asleep yet? I've been singing for many years.

The Daughter said: *I'm not sleepy Mother. Can you bring me water?*

The Mother brought water.

Then the Daughter asked the Mother to help her get cozy again.

So the Mother fluffed up the cloud pillows and smoothed out the hillside and cooled the area more for the Daughter so that she would fall asleep.

Mother, would you sing again?

So the Mother started singing again.

Nights like this happened throughout the Daughter's early eons, and the Mother never told the Daughter she was exhausted from all the singing and that there were times it was the birds and unicorns who were singing in place of the Mother — their combined singing was the sound most similar to the Mother's voice that her creatures could produce. The Daughter never knew and the Mother never told her.

Much later the Daughter would seek adventures across the Orb in low places, secret places, and deep places. She even went through a period of helping the dog-god find much of the magic the cat-god had hidden. She found the most magic at the center of the Orb, buried way deep inside the Mother. She approached the magic and felt the burning heat as the magic twisted and turned, flowed like rivers, and ascended up through the Mother to her surface. The Mother just smiled, watching her Daughter explore and have her adventures with her dog-god nearby and her cat-god watching over them both and acting when needed.

The cat-god found it annoying that they found the magic she had so carefully hidden, but she so loved the Daughter she did not arch her back or anything. She simply waited for the dog-god and Daughter to sleep or get distracted and then she'd hide much of the magic again; but, like her Goddess, she always left some out where the Daughter would find it, because the cat-god secretly enjoyed playing with the Daughter. She would let her know one day soon. Perhaps in five-hundred thousand years or so.

One time the Daughter was playing with the unicorns, and the Woodland Elves invited her to sit and have tea with them and their queen. The Daughter was delighted, of course, and she and the dog-god enjoyed a nice tea with the Elf Queen and her retinue. The Elf Queen asked about her Mother — for the Elf Queen was the Mother's oldest friend and their stories and adventures rivaled the Daughter's, and so the Daughter often sought out the Queen to hear the stories and adventures of her Mother. She'd tell her Mother what the Queen said and her Mother would just reply: *Did she tell you that? Oh dear, well, the story is a little different, of course; it was not an "evil" Being we banished; none of my creation is evil, some are just more ill-tempered than others and, well, the creature needed a timeout.*

But Mother, the Daughter said, *the Queen said there was a great battle in the sky, and the creatures all scrambled and the sky was torn, and the Queen had to summon all her nation to a great battle at your side; and there were other Gods from other Universes — giant evil Gods who were jealous of you and your Creation!*

Oh, my goodness, Daughter! I must talk to my friend! She is the first Queen, my dear friend, and companion, my long time love, and first among all creatures who helped sustain my garden during and before it was actually a garden. And she exaggerates our adventures.

She went on: *There were mild disagreements with some visiting Gods who wanted to see the Goddess' universe and they overstayed their welcome — Gods tend to do that, so I usually have very strict visiting rules — seven-hundred million years maximum, and everyone has to leave — so, I politely asked them to leave, and they did.*

Then why was the Elf Queen there? the Daughter asked.

Well, the Goddess said, *she knew I grew impatient and so technically it was she who asked them to leave while I tended my garden.*

The Daughter thought there was more to this story. She would ask her

Mother again one day.

While the Daughter was with the Elf Queen, she learned more about the nature of magic, magic objects and, her favorite, fairies. The fairies were fun and kind and played all day and danced and sang all night and the Daughter loved them! They were young beings on the Orb, for they had only been around a few billion years and the Elves called them "children" because they were so young. That word, children, was eventually transferred to creatures who looked like the Daughter, because that is what the Daughter called them, in honor of her fairy friends.

The fairies were just so hard to find, for their lands disappeared at night and reappeared in the morning in a different location. The Mother said it was because the fairies needed to spread the flower seeds and thus they needed to follow the seasons. And they only slept for a few hours a night, *like the Daughter*, the Mother thought.

One time, the dog-god took the Daughter to one of her favorite valleys where she had dug up large holes and made large mounds. After running up and sliding down the mounds, the Daughter saw flowers and decided she wanted to be an artist, like her Mother.

So, she gathered up as many flowers as she could, in as many colors as she could find, and she held them to the dog-god's nose and let her wet nose cause the colors to run off the flowers into the Daughter's hands. With her colored hands the Daughter started coloring the side of the hill with beautiful illustrations of flowers, the Sun, the dog-god, some fairies, her friends the Elves, and some mountains. And in the center of the drawing was her picture of the Mother.

It was the first image of the Mother.

In the drawing, the Mother was very tall. Her hair was blacker than deep space and there were streaks of lightning in her thick, twisted hair that never stopped moving. Her eyes were large, and wide, and her eye color was a color not found in the garden and neither in the colors the Mother left in the sky. Her cheekbones were smooth and round, and the Mother's hands were soft and, though the Daughter did not draw this, she knew they smelled of cherry-almond.

The Mother wore no clothes in her garden or ever, for she was the Mother and the Orb was her clothing, so she wore no clothing in the Daughter's picture. In the drawing, the Mother held the Sun in her hand and the Moon shone just over her shoulder. Her arms were stretched out over the Orb and just over there, on the bottom left, was a picture of the Daughter looking up at, and in love with, the Mother.

The Daughter was proud of her art and so she asked the dog-god to bring it with them so she could give it to her Mother.

She presented the drawing to her Mother and the Mother gasped, for she had never seen herself through her Daughter's eyes — though she could have had she chosen to.

It was beautiful art, and the Mother cried more tears of joy at her Daughter's art.

Daughter, this is a beautiful work of art and drawing! Aren't you the artist!

The Daughter beamed and the dog-god smiled and wagged its tail, feeling that maybe, just maybe, she knew who was a good dog.

The cat-god was also impressed. But she kept it to herself — although she wrapped her tail around the Daughter to show her approval. The

Daughter knew that the cat-god was proud even before she felt the tail around her leg.

Then the Mother said: *We will hang your drawing in our garden so that we may see it every day. I love you and I love your art. Thank you, Daughter.*

The Daughter repeated her drawings almost every day for the next three-hundred years and soon the garden was running out of places to hang all her drawings.

One time, the Daughter was gone for a bit too long. She was out exploring as she often did. The Mother called her to come home: *Daughter, it is time to come in.*

I don't want to come in yet, Mother, I'm still playing.

They continued like this for ten or so years before finally the Mother went to the Daughter who was high atop a mountain where it was snowing and she had been playing with the snow creatures.

Daughter, why are you ignoring me? Come on, we're going home to our garden.

Mother, I'm not ready. Please, just a few more years!

The Mother said, *Okay, just a few more. I'll wait here.*

The Mother waited. And waited. And then when thirty years had passed she said:

Daughter, get your things. We are going home right now. The Daughter hesitated and barely moved. The Mother was patient — she had created a universe and all things in it after all.

But this! This was too much, she thought. She said again: *We are leaving. Now.* All the snow creatures had disappeared into the snow at the Mother's voice. The Daughter sat still for another few years.

The snow was now melting, but just around the Mother.

Mother, the Daughter finally spoke, *I have achieved Enlightenment.*

The Mother stared. And then smiled. *Daughter, why didn't you say that was what you were doing? I hid Enlightenment here and a few other places for later — much later. How did you find it?*

Mother, the daughter replied, *one does not find Enlightenment; Enlightenment comes where it is accepted.*

And the Mother marveled at her Daughter.

And then she swooped her into her arms and they went home.

* * *

After a few more instances of the Daughter not coming home and/or not wanting to leave her latest endeavor, the Mother made the Three Rules for play and for when they attended special events, such as the many Elven celebrations, to watch a new star being born, a new galaxy collision, or to watch the Orb give birth time and again.

The Three Rules were:

1. Always have fun.

2. No one cries unless they get hurt (their feelings hurt).

3. When it's time to go, it's time to go.

It took an eon or two to firmly establish the Three Rules but the Daughter seemed to like a little bit of structure and so the rules tended to work very well.

Except when they didn't work and the Mother had to start over.

Which she did not mind.

Unless she did.

The Daughter was growing up and the Mother loved watching her grow, learn more art, and make their garden a little more beautiful every millenia.

PROCESS

Creation is merely the process of growing up.

Mother, the Daughter called.

Yes, darling, the Mother replied.

Why are the other beings fighting?

The Daughter had seen fighting before, of course. As civilizations grew and grew they began fighting one another. She'd watch and try to understand as best she could and she would watch as the fighter groups stopped fighting.

But this fighting was different and so she asked her Mother.

The Mother knew this day would arrive. The Daughter had explored the entirety of the Orb multiple times, and she'd watched the other beings — the Daughter called them "babies" because they were so young, unpredictable, sweet, mean, and very wild. She lived among them and when she did she made sure she looked like one of them so that she could go unnoticed. She traveled all over the Orb and lived amongst many different baby civilizations and she loved them all, differently.

She'd stay for a brief moment or few hundred years before moving on to another civilization. And when she'd return after a few thousand years, she'd see all the changes they made and how they'd grown, and she'd view their art, which always came first; how they started using tools, and how they Ended. The Endings were always sad to the Daughter even though they all returned to the Mother and were instantly greeted and celebrated by the Mother.

Round and round the world the Daughter traveled and at every stop she taught civilization how to live, love, laugh, play, and care for all the plants, trees, and of course all the creatures, especially the dogs and cats. The dog-god and cat-god traveled with her and made sure to look in on all their babies, too.

She made sure never to be too prominent in their societies but sometimes after she left, movements were started that worshiped her. She paid no attention to the movements except when she shared tiny bits of magic with some of her sisters who worshipped her. The magic was small and usually a brief storm, or more crops grown, or healing a baby or visiting with a sick person before their Ending. Those were the hardest for her, but they also brought the most joy, so she did millions of those.

And the Daughter also brought creatures home with her. All the time. Small, large, swimmers, fliers, crawlers, and on and on. The Mother allowed them, of course, because they were her beings. And there were so many! She started removing a few every time the Daughter brought more home but the Daughter noticed, of course, and just brought them back. So the Mother set aside space on all the continents just for creatures and she told the Daughter to visit them often; and the Daughter did just that. And she brought more home.

And the Daughter brought other friends home, too, from the civilizations she visited, and they visited her home and marveled at the garden and how she lived with so many animals that were wild and dangerous! But the Daughter just laughed and they usually enjoyed tea, fruit, seeds, and plants. The Daughter shared stories and jokes, observations, and every now and then she gave advice. She tried to avoid giving advice but her friends begged her and so she would eventually give in. They'd leave and when they returned to their homes they'd realize they had been gone many years and that while they were the same age, their families had aged considerably during the one or two days they were gone. It was for this reason the Daughter seldom brought friends home to her and the

Mother's garden.

Upon leaving, many tried to remember everything the Daughter had told them but most of the time they forgot. But they would talk to one another and piece together their different memories, and through those gatherings they put some of the Daughter's writings in a book and shared it with their other family and associates. While the book was many pages long and held fantastical stories, songs, and sayings that they believed the Daughter said herself, the book was called different things in different parts of the Orb and was slightly different in each version. The book was called *The Daughter's Holy Words,* or *The First Book of the Daughter,* or *The Daughter* or, simply *Daughter.* Each book was slightly different and those who loved the Daughter found no argument or disagreement in their different words or interpretations of her words. They all loved her and loved exploring new and different views of who she was and what she meant to them.

The Daughter laughed at the titles, thinking it was a bit too much to call her stories and sayings holy. The Goddess was holy, and the Mother. She was the Daughter and that was enough, she thought. The only thing she forbade was anyone calling her Goddess. She was not Goddess, the Goddess was Goddess, now and forever. Some insisted but she would not hear it because while she was First Born of the Mother, and Daughter to the Goddess, and she alone could be in the Goddess' presence, she was the Daughter. The different groups who had different names for their book debated endlessly about the nature of Goddess and Daughter and Mother and whether they were all the same, or two, or three, or even more. These discussions and debates never ceased for many generations, and all the while the Daughter was very clear: I am the Daughter. The Goddess created all things and I am her Daughter. The Mother is Mother to us all and I am the First Born of the Mother.

And still they debated as they read her words over and over through many generations. The books of the Daughter's words had thousands of pages but could be summed up thusly:

1. Be kind to one another at all times.

2. Be kind to all creatures, large and small – never eat them!

3. When the Mother calls you, answer.

4. Seek your friends for they are seeking you.

5. Be kind to the trees, the oceans, and the mountains, and tend your garden.

6. Never put a dragonfly and a firefly in the same area. (No one ever understood this one.)

7. Seek the Goddess.

8. Do not stare into the eyes of a cat for too long or you will be lost.

9. Always ask the dog-god: *Who is a good dog?*

10. Smell your mother's hair as often as you can. (Philosophers forever debate this one.)

The civilizations now had large cities, great boats, and greater structures, beautiful art and a few hundred-thousand languages. The daughter loved seeing all the sights and soon she made friends with other daughters who were actually her sisters, since they also were from the Mother, but none of them realized it. By this time, some civilizations began teaching things that were different than the truth.

The Daughter listened to the stories told by leaders who said they spoke for god and told the people when god was happy, or mad, or when god wanted war, or when god wanted obedience or tributes.

The Goddess and Mother wanted none of those things.

Silly children, the Daughter thought. She knew what the Mother wanted, for the Mother told her.

All the time.

In fact, the Daughter often wished her Mother would stop telling her the same things over and over. The Mother said it was so she would learn because one day she would need to know all these things so that she could tell her own Daughters.

The Daughter laughed at her Mother's funny jokes.

Finally the Mother answered her Daughter's question about why the beings were fighting.

Daughter, she started, *they are fighting because they misunderstand. They seek to know, and often they find answers and misuse the answers for their own gain. And so they argue, and arguing can lead to fighting, and fighting can lead to Endings.*

The Daughter was quiet. She listened to the Mother. And as she listened, the Mother took her on a trip that lasted thousands of years and that looked in on many villages, cities, regions, city-states, countries, and nations as their fighting started small and then grew, and grew, and grew until there was fighting all over the Orb.

So the Mother and Daughter traveled around the Orb and visited all the civilizations. And while they did they spoke in their own quiet language that sounded like singing wind.

The Mother said: *They fight about creation and whether it is real.*

The Daughter replied: *But your Creation is beautiful and real!*

The Mother said: *They fight about the meaning and nature of god.*

The Daughter replied: *But the Goddess is perfect and the Mother shows her perfection.*

The Mother said: *They fight about who is god, this one or that one?*

The Daughter replied: *But the Goddess is God and Creator of all.*

The Mother said: *They fight about land and property.*

The Daughter replied: *But the Orb is too big for them; there's room for all!*

The Mother said: *They fight about resources: water, air, and minerals.*

The Daughter replied: *But the Mother has more than enough for everyone!*

The Mother said: *They fight about food.*

The Daughter replied: *But the garden from the beginning is never bare!*

The Mother said: *They fight about wealth and gold and money.*

The Daughter replied: *But those things belong to the Orb and besides, those things are silly.*

The Mother said: *They fight about creatures.*

The Daughter replied: *And they end them and EAT them — my babies!*

The Daughter had tears now.

The Mother said: *They fight about borders.*

The Daughter replied: *But you didn't make borders; all the land is free!*

The Mother said: *They fight about medicine.*

The Daughter replied: *But your garden provides enough medicine for everyone!*

The Mother said: *They fight about which religion is the only true religion.*

The Daughter replied: *But the Goddess loves them all the same.*

The Mother said: *They fight about who sins the most.*

The Daughter replied: *Well, that would be me, but you teach forgiveness.* (The Mother smiled at her Daughter's honesty.)

The Mother said: *They fight about sex.*

The Daughter replied: *Mother!*

The Mother said: *Ok, they fight about love.*

The Daughter replied: *But you teach that love is love!*

The Mother said: *They fight about the roles of your sisters.*

The Daughter replied: *They call them witch and enchantress as if those are bad things!*

The Mother said: *They fight about witchcraft and sorcery.*

The Daughter replied: *But the witches were here before them and are my friends!*

The Mother said: *They fight about all the colors I gave them for their bodies.*

The Daughter replied: *But all Creation is from you and from you are all colors!*

The Mother said: *They fight about heaven and hell.*

The Daughter replied: *But there is no hell; only the loving arms of the Mother,* which is *Heaven!*

And when they had visited all the civilizations on the Orb, the Daughter had come to her fullness, and better understood what civilization meant. She understood evil, and religion, and war, famine, disease, anger, murder, abuse, lies, drug addiction, hurt, depravity, hunger, and manipulations.

And the civilizations had spread over the Orb, which they mistakenly called "Earth." And the great cities were now full with millions of beings and they stopped caring for the gardens of the Orb. And they muddied the waters and oceans. The skies were full of dirt and where there was no dirt there was sickness in the aura the Goddess placed around the Orb to protect it from the other creations in her Universe.

And the fighting that so concerned the Daughter now raged day and night with misuse of the Orb's materials, and the fighting spanned the entirety of the Orb, never ceasing. And the Daughter's sisters were hidden and fearful. They were cast out and hunted and labeled witches and whores, heretics and evildoers, and spawn of evil and demons of false gods. The witches hid and took with them many of their sisters of the Orb: the magicians, the Wiccans, the sorceress, the tarot readers, the crones, the intuitionists, the diviners, the mind readers, and alchemists, the doctors and teachers, the lovers of themselves, the leaders, the vocal, the single, those with many children, and those with none, those who refused to have children, and the midwives who brought children to life.

And many more followed the witches and they had one thing in common: All were like the Daughter, and her sisters.

The Daughter wept.

She wept for her sisters.

She wept for the Elves who had hidden deep within the Mother and had taken all the magical beings with them to protect them. She wept for the trees and for the minerals of the Orb. She wept for the oceans and the things that swam. She wept for the birds, the dogs and cats who were hungry and alone. She wept for the forests and beaches, and for the plains, and deserts because none could escape the fury of the humans, as she now called them.

They were no longer babies.

And mostly, she wept for the Goddess and Mother, who saw this small part of her creation forget her benevolence and love; who perverted their understanding and twisted the meaning of god and eliminated the Goddess Mother from all their beliefs.

And she looked at the Mother who stood resolute. And she thought back billions of years to her first drawing of the Mother and how young she, the Daughter was, and how accurate her drawing was.

For here stood the Mother Goddess. Resplendent. In glory. The Sun in her hand. The Moon over her shoulder. Her hair thick and twisted like deep space with streaks of lightning. Her countenance overwhelming for all but the Daughter.

The Mother Goddess smelled of cherry-almond and the Daughter took all of the Mother Goddess in.

The Mother Goddess did not often assume this form. But this moment she did. And she was and is and always will be the source of all love and beauty in her Universe.

She was the Goddess Mother.

And all Creation took notice.

And the Daughter reached out to her. First Born of the Mother Goddess to the First Born of Creation to the Creator of all things.

And the Daughter knew. The Daughter's time had come and she welcomed it.

LOVE

Creation is merely and always an act of love.

Mother, I know what I have to do, the Daughter said.

The Goddess Mother was still. *You are ready, my Daughter. And my Orb is ready. I am with you.*

The Daughter considered her Mother. She had always been her Mother. And she had always been her Goddess. She was the Goddess Mother, Creator of all things. Sustainer of all her Creation and First of all Creations everywhere in all universes, past, present, and future.

No one had ever seen the Goddess Mother in her glory or true form, except the Daughter.

The Daughter considered the Goddess Mother and loved her. She loved her garden, and her creatures, and her planets and galaxies, and atoms, and black holes, and singularities, and protons and neutrons, and mountains, and rain.

She so loved her rain!

And she loved her wisdom and her stories. She loved her jokes and how she laughed. She loved when she talked to the Sun and laughed with the Moon deep into the night. She loved when the Elf Queen visited and the Goddess Mother allowed her to listen to them talk in a language only the three of them understood. And she marveled at their love for one another and how caring and loving they were to and with each other. And she laughed at their discussions and debates over silly things like why the Goddess created an event horizon at the edge of black holes, or why there was a speed limit in her Universe, or why Matter and dark matter acted strangely or why she played tricks with time travel! They debated causality and the strangeness of the quantum world and micro-universes. (The Goddess simply said: *Art goes where it will.*)

They carried on heated discussions about which flower was prettiest and which tree was best, which fruit was sweetest (watermelon always won), and why she made so many different animals. What could she have possibly been thinking when she made the badger, or skunk, or lobster, or wombat, or anteater?

They discussed, disagreed, and debated for years and years over these same topics that never had a resolution.

They loved one another and were partners in all things. The Daughter wished that type of love for all the creatures on the Orb. But it was not to be.

And now the Daughter took her final form. She had many forms that allowed her to settle into all civilizations and all places. She did not have a favorite size, or color, or look — she loved all her forms. Civilization had many names for her, many hundreds of names. None were her true name though, and none captured her true form as Daughter.

For this task she settled her form so that it would send a message to the humans.

She would be Everything. And Every Daughter. She would have long hair. And short hair, curly hair, and straight hair. She would wear an Afro, and she would wear her hair straight down her back. And she would wear all her curls in full chaos beauty. She would have black, brown, gold, red, grey, and many other colors of hair. She would be bald. And she would wear a hijab that covered her hair, and she would wear a niqab that covered her hair and only showed her eyes. Henna was on her hands.

And her henna told of her love for the Goddess and Mother, her love for the Elf Queen, the cat-god and dog-god, and for all her friends and creatures. The Daughter's henna was the original henna from which all henna flowed on all sisters even until now.

The Daughter was tall and her usual color was the color of coffee, with just enough cream so that she was sun-kissed about her face. All versions that showed her hair would now show it wrapped in colorful strings with gems sprinkled here and there; and she had multi-colored silk tied into her thick twists — the thick twists were in honor of her Mother; and the scarves of many colors were also in honor of her Mother's streak of lightning in her own hair and the curved colors in the sky.

She was as close an approximation of the Goddess, in one form, as anyone would ever see or be allowed to see.

The Daughter's eyes settled to a darker than light brown, and behind them the Sun rested; and the Moon was in her hands.

She sent love to her Goddess Mother and said simply: It is time.

The Goddess Mother blessed her and said: Go forth — You are my Daughter.

And the Daughter first called her sisters to her. The sound shocked the humans and all the lands trembled at the sound of the Daughter's call to her sisters.

All the daughters, all the witches, and all their sisters recognized the Daughter's voice and rejoiced. And out of the dark places, and light places, and out of the caves and forests, out of the great cities, and slums, and out of the hospitals and drug dens, and out of the fields, and prisons, and out of the industry, they heard their sister the Daughter and they came to her from all over the Orb.

The world trembled and the armies of humans found common cause to cease their wars to join together against what was coming.

The leaders of human government and their armies gathered with the religious leaders and reached agreement: Evil had arrived and the Great Whore was here to destroy the age of science, technology, and civilization. The human governments, religions, and their armies must unite and destroy her, they all decided and agreed.

And so the call went out to all the earth to gather all armies and all able bodies to unite to fight the Great Whore and the Great Evil.

Millions answered the call of the human leaders. Then Billions. They gathered all over the earth and brought their weapons of war with them and they prepared for what they called the Final Battle.

The Daughter welcomed her sisters with tea, ice cream, chocolate, stories, laughter, and love. The land smelled of cherry-almond. The sisters didn't bring weapons or hate or anger. Not even the woman warriors from the secret island. They, as did every sister, brought love. And they loved the Daughter and she loved them back and shared the love from the Mother Goddess. They came by the millions. And then billions. And they were every creature, and every type of being on the Orb. Magical, legendary and myths, all came to the Daughter. And all the animals and beasts heard the Daughter's call and went to her and loved her. And she loved them back. All came, large and small, swimmers and fliers. And the dragonflies and fireflies, which celebrated their reunion after millennia, looked forward to again becoming dragons.

And cats and dogs came, led by the cat-god and dog-god. Billions of cats and dogs followed their cat-god and dog-god to the Daughter. And she loved them all and they loved her back, even the cats. And the cat-god settled next to the Daughter and started purring and all the cats purred their love to the cat-god and she transferred their love and energy to the Daughter.

And all the dogs and wolves howled and barked in celebration. For they had finally found their answer to the eternal question they long sought: *Who's a good dog?* For the answer came from the Daughter herself who said to the gathered dogs who were lined up behind the dog-god: *Where are all my good dogs? Here you all are! You are all good dogs! Come to your Daughter.*

And the dogs loved the Daughter and she loved them back.

Then the Daughter asked the Orb to send to her all the sisters who were sleeping in the Orb, in the ground and in the oceans — those early daughters who were asleep for millions of years and the daughters who went to sleep in the last few minutes. And the Orb woke all the sleeping sisters and sent them to the Daughter.

And then the Daughter called for all the helpers to come to her. These were daughters and sons who also loved the Goddess Mother even when they weren't quite sure there was a Goddess Mother. They were called to the Daughter because they treated the Orb with love; they protected the weak and they cared for the creatures. They healed the land and protected the water, and air, and flowers. They were caretakers, artists, poets, singers, writers, teachers, musicians, lovers, babies, grandmothers, aunts, and nieces, and all of the Divine Feminine.

They all came to the Daughter and she welcomed them, women, girls, men, and boys. And they understood and loved her back.

Now the armies of civilization were gathered all over the Orb and they were ready. They had been watching and listening from the sky as the Daughter gathered her army and they also watched from land and sea and they planned to soon attack from all those places so that they would surprise what they called the Great Evil and the Great Whore.

The time of the Final Battle had come.

The attacks started when the Sun went down one beautiful evening. The attacks first came from the sky as unseen super fast flying machines dropped thousand upon thousands of great bombs. And even faster machines dropped even more bombs.

At the same time, the Daughter had gathered all the fireflies and dragonflies to either side of her.

She spoke and said: *Please, unite.*

And there was a great buzz as the insects swirled and swirled around the Daughter in celebration — For they would be whole again!

In a few moments the fireflies and dragonflies were gone, and in their place rested dragons by the thousands. They were magnificent in their terror and beautiful in their colors.

Their eyes shone forth to the gathered sisters and creatures, and in their eyes was the fire of love for their Daughter and their Goddess. All the gathered were silent in reverence to the magnificent creatures that were so loved by the Goddess and Daughter, and so feared by the humans.

And then the dragon wings started flapping and mighty roars filled the air in celebration and shook the Orb in faraway places, even to the gathered government and religious leaders.

Then the Daughter said, *Dragon Queen, come to me.*

And the dragons quieted and parted. And the Dragon Queen approached the Daughter. She was bigger in size than the human's flying machines.

She was many colors of purple. She was beautiful. She was regal. She was what the humans called a horror. But the Dragon Queen was created by the Goddess for just this time and place and like all of the Goddess' creations, she was beautiful and full of love for the Goddess Mother and the Daughter.

The Dragon Queen approached the Daughter and said: *Daughter, it is good to see you. You have your Mother's eyes.*

And the Daughter bowed to the Dragon Queen and said, *thank you, Queen and Sister. Mother says hello and asked that you visit her deep inside her and ignite a fire. And also, would you be so kind as to ask your dragons to disperse those things that are about to fall on us?*

The Dragon Queen looked up. Fire now covered her lavender colored eyes and she spoke to her thousands of dragons. Her language was the sound of an approaching earthquake. And the dragon hoard responded in kind.

And then, silence.

And then thousands upon thousands of dragons took to the air in resplendent colors that mirrored the many colors of the gardens they had tended for the Goddess all these millennia.

Thousands of dragons in whose belly the oldest fires lived released their fire in great streaks that burned bomb after bomb, causing them to explode in the air, and the dragons fed on what was left of them. The skies were filled with explosions that were met with all the colors of dragon fire and a dragon feeding festival that colored the sky and made the Daughter and her sisters and creatures laugh and smile in wonder at the magnificent art of the dragons.

The dragons were whole again, now and forever, and they thanked the Daughter, who had eyes like her mother, for reuniting them. And they continued burning the falling bombs out of the air and the gathered sisters could hear what sounded like playing and laughing from the dragons as they flew through the air, twirling this way and that, while bombs exploded all around them, by their own doing, and they bathed in the explosions which tickled them.

And the Dragon Queen flew into the largest volcano on the Orb and she descended hundreds of miles into its belly to her former home. The Mother welcomed her and they communed before the dragon remembered her task.

The Queen of all dragons, friend of the Goddess, lover of the Orb, and soon to be owner of all her gold again, discharged a great and mighty purple dragon flame deeper into the Mother.

And the Mother groaned. And then the dragon fire turned upwards and ignited the rocks that lined the walls of the volcano. And then the Dragon Queen, satisfied, took to the air leading the explosion of purple flames of lava out of the volcano. The sight was impossible but happening and the world's leaders turned to the giant volcano and witnessed a beautiful miracle that was terrifying to them.

The Dragon Queen flew out of the Volcano and into the sky and purple lava flames trailed her, and immediately there was an explosion that shook the Orb as the Mother released so much energy that had lain asleep in this one volcano. The dragons, who had finished eating all the bombs, were in a frenzy seeing their Queen lead the holy flame into the sky that burned up the large flying machines as they dropped their final bombs.

The skies were soon cleared of all flying machines and their bombs.

The armies reconsidered.

Next they attacked from the oceans thousands of miles away. They turned their great battle boats to face the area where the Daughter had gathered her army and then just as they were set to launch their attacks the ocean began turning this way and that.

For the Daughter had visited the ocean and asked the ocean creatures to help her to clear the waters again. The Great Whale, the queen of all the oceans, heard the Daughter's plea and responded.

The Great Whale Queen said, *Daughter, please say hello to the Goddess and let her know we miss her and to please visit soon.* The Daughter said she would let her Goddess know.

And then the great Whale Queen said: *Daughter, I at first thought you were the Goddess, you have your Mother's voice.*

And the Daughter was gracious and thanked the Whale Queen for the compliment. (And thought, *do I really sound so much like Mother?*)

Then the Daughter said, *Great Whale Queen and Sister, would you be so kind and prevent these war machines from harming my sisters and creatures gathered over there?*

The Whale Queen replied: *Of course, Daughter. See you soon.*

And then the massive battle boats were pushed around by giant whales who pushed the boats away from where they drifted and turned them away from their targets. The great engines of war boats were no match for the hundreds of thousands of great whales. Many of the whales were awakened by the Orb and were the same whales who had been slaughtered for thousands of years by the humans. The whales slowly moved this way and that as they shoved the battle boats this way and that while they celebrated clearing their waters of the awful machines.

Today was the day that these giant beautiful creatures were created for, to shove the awful giant boats out of the way for the Daughter and her sisters.

And for the soldiers who fell into the water, the Great Whale Queen sent more whales, dolphins, seals, sharks, and other great sea animals — not to eat them, but to keep the fallen warriors from being drowned.

Next came the soldiers on the ground who had been notified by the spies that now was the time to attack because the Great Evil and her demons were dancing.

And attack they did, in great steel machines and with great long-range weapons and bombs. The soldiers used technology that allowed them to see in the dark. What they didn't see were the thousands upon thousands of cats staring at them in the dark. The cat-god had been waiting patiently as her cats came from all over the Orb, from shelters, and from the wild plains. As they arrived, small cats and extremely large cats with mighty roars, spotted coats, black coats, streaky coats, and more, each paid tribute to the cat-god and took their places where the soldiers could not see them.

The cat-god and her cats did not need technology to see in the dark or to sneak up on anything. They were cats. This is what they were created for, this very moment.

When the soldiers thought they were surprising the Daughter's sisters and creatures, the cats had been watching them all along in the dark, so that as soon as the armies started moving, the millions of cats started their attack.

The attack by the cats so startled the soldiers that they started running from the great cat-god and her gigantic cats who unleashed mighty roars that shook the trees. Running was just what the cats wanted the armies to do, for the dog-god loved to chase things. And catch things. And shake things this way and that in her sharp teeth before throwing things way away from her.

The dog-god and the dogs and wolves had been created for just this moment.

When the soldiers began running, the dogs began howling and started chasing them, following the lead of the dog-god who was now fierce and running like the wind. She was happy because she had so much to chase and when she caught her prey, she simply tossed them aside like a toy and made sure they were asleep before moving on to more prey. The dog-god commanded the same of the wolves and the wolves suppressed their desire for revenge because they loved the dog-god and so they copied her and sought her approval. There were millions of dogs and wolves and they had waited patiently for the soldiers to attack. And now they were having more fun than they'd ever had and they loved the dog-god and Daughter for giving them so many things to chase, catch, toss, chase some more, toss a few more times high in the air, and to have so much fun.

But not only the dogs, but the creatures of old were also there: The elephants and rhinos, the bulls and bison, and there were even pre-human creatures from the early life on the Orb – the dinosaurs who had been asleep so long they were groggy and hungry. They saw the giant steel machines and they loved the Daughter for giving them big slow food! The Daughter came to them and asked they that just crack the shells and let the dogs and wolves do the rest; she promised them big food later. Plants. They would get plants, the Daughter told herself, and no one would ever eat her creatures again.

And so the great ancient creatures, the dogs and wolves, and the many other creatures played with the attacking armies for many days and months without ceasing and the armies never reached the Daughter or her friends.

The government and religious leaders monitored and saw what was happening and instead of loving the Daughter they decided to launch their most terrible weapons. The religious leaders and government leaders were all in agreement: send the full arsenal to defeat the Great Whore and all her evil followers.

First, there was silence. And then, great streaks lined the sky as the most terrible weapons launched from air, sea, low orbit, and land.

The Orb said to the Daughter: *Daughter, be a dear and please handle those attacks. I don't want to ruin the Goddess' garden. Be a Daughter, and protect me.*

And the Daughter replied: *I love you, Orb. I will protect Mother's garden. And all my paintings*, she thought.

The Daughter then felt something deep inside her, and looked to see the Elf Queen, who was crying.

The Daughter walked to her and, laying one hand on her beautiful beyond-dark hair, the Daughter asked: *My Queen, what troubles you this joyous night of song and dance?*

The ancient Elf Queen just smiled for a moment. Her tears were not of fear for the Daughter. Her tears were the tears of a proud step-parent. For the Elf Queen had known the Daughter from infancy to now, with the Daughter in the fullness of Womanhood.

You have grown into a lovely woman and it all happened so fast, she thought.

The Elf Queen had helped raise her as one of her own — and she had thousands of daughters and sons herself. The Goddess Mother had fully entrusted her First Born of the Orb to her friend and lover the Elf Queen and she had never been more proud as a parent than in this moment. She welcomed the Daughter, her Daughter, into her arms and she held her, as she did when she was a young girl spending centuries in the forest. She smelled her hair, and it smelled like the Goddess Mother, cherry-almond but with a dash of dog-god and cat-god breath and Elfin forest.

She loved her Daughter and her Daughter loved her back.

Then her Daughter said: *I love you, Mamma, and the Elf Queen fully cried tears of joy and the Elfin nation cried with her and remembered this moment forever and ever as the day the Elf Queen officially adopted the First Born Daughter.*

The Elf Queen then said: *Be the Daughter your Mother raised.* And the Daughter said: *I will be the Daughter that you and Mother raised, Mamma.* And they kissed, Mamma and Daughter, embraced for all the gathered to see, and all were in tears as colorful light embraced them and then the words of the Goddess sounded:

In my Daughter is all my love for Creation; And in the Elf Queen all my love for my Daughter is Entrusted. Behold! My Loves!

And the Universe trembled and humbled itself before its Creator.

And the Elf Queen said: *Go, Daughter, your Mothers are with you, always.*

Then the Daughter left the gathering and turned her face upward.

She first paid tribute to the Wind. And the Wind howled back.

Next she asked the Orb to flip her magnetic field. The Orb did that on occasion just to play tricks on her children.

The flipped magnetic field caused the great long-range bombs to lose their navigation systems and fly aimlessly in the air.

Then the Daughter asked the clouds to cover the Moon and cover the Orb.

And the clouds agreed and covered the Orb all around causing the great lasers in the sky to lose their targets and wait for the clouds to disperse.

Then the Daughter turned to the Sun and greeted the Sun as a sibling, sending her love. The Sun loved her back and asked what she could do to help.

Great Sister Sun, I will ask the clouds to part, and when they do, the great flying bombs will find their targets and start heading toward all my sisters. These bombs are even too terrible for my Dragon Queen. Would you be so kind as to prevent them from landing on our heads? It would badly ruin our tea and our dancing and we are not quite finished. And Mother doesn't want them to ruin her garden.

The Sun swelled with pride and honor. She loved her sister and she had waited billions of years for this request. She thought back to the Goddess being so kind to her, and she winked fire at her sister the Moon.

And the Daughter asked the clouds to part, and they did. And at the same time the great missiles in the sky regrouped and found their targets and headed in the direction of the Daughter and her sisters and her creatures.

The government and religious leaders of the civilizations started to celebrate as they believed their greatest weapons would soon kill the Great Whore, her followers, and even the earth. They were proud of the coming destruction of billions of humans and trillions of creatures, plants and gardens. This was why the humans had created all their weapons – to destroy all that they could in the name of their gods, their technology, and their science.

The Sun was ready. She directed her attention to the flying bombs and then she directed her energy in a massive Sun flare that traveled at the speed limit the Goddess set (*why did she do that?* the Sun wondered) and in an instant the flares reached all the great flying bombs and incinerated them in the air. And for good measure, the Sun sent Sun flares to the great orbiting machines, and her Sun flares instantly knocked out all of their great communication systems and those same systems on the Orb, leaving the great masses of civilizations unable to communicate across great distances.

The explosions of the giant flying bombs were beyond anything any of the Daughter's sisters had ever seen; and bigger and more terrible than anyone had seen ever, in all the wars of civilization from the dawn of civilization.

This war was the Final War, and the war all other earth wars had been leading up to.

There was fallout from the great flying bombs and the Daughter had anticipated the fallout and she knew what would happen should the fallout reach the Orb.

So the Daughter asked some of the secret little things — particles, elements, bacteria, atoms, and smaller things that are family with Matter and other secret things more ancient than all things, even the Elves — to protect her creatures and sisters. They were there at the beginning with the Goddess and they had explored secret multiverses and micro verses and the quantum world where the Goddess sometimes played.

Secret things, the Daughter started, *would you be so kind and protect my sisters and creatures from the fallout of those great bombs?*

And the secret things rejoiced for they loved the Daughter and knew of her coming from the beginning of this universe. They sent their love to the Daughter, and to the Goddess, and the Daughter returned their love.

Then the little things said: *Hello Daughter, we love you and miss you and our Goddess. Please ask her to come play with us. And you please join her. Also, your aura is like the Goddess, and we thought you were her.*

The Daughter thanked them for their compliment and invitation and she promised to visit soon. (And thought: *my, now even my aura is like my Mother's?*)

And so the secret things saw the fallout and went to the fallout and changed the radiation and poison and other radioactive tiny things into flowers. Their abilities to change and manipulate matter was one of the hidden secrets the Goddess placed on the Orb that the civilizations could have found if they had focused on living and discovering and protecting the Orb instead of killing and destroying the Orb.

And so flowers rained down on the party of all the gathered sisters, helpers, and creatures, and the Daughter laughed a joyous laugh and the Sun said to her: *Daughter, you laugh with the sound of your Mother.* Everyone laughed and she did as well because she loved her Mother. (She also laughed to herself and accepted that she was, in fact, just like her Mother in many ways and that was a wonderful thing.)

The leaders of the humans, the governments and religious leaders and others were angrier than ever that their attacks caused no harm to the Great Harlot. They conferred and determined their final attacks.

Now on the part of the Orb where the Daughter was, it was early morning and all the witches and humans and magical beings were just waking up because the birds would not stop singing. But their song today was different from how it had been over the past few months and years. It was louder, if that were possible, and celebratory.

Once everyone was awake, they switched to singing a version of the Goddess Song that the Goddess sang when she wanted the Daughter to sleep. The unicorns joined in and even though everyone had just awakened, everyone was now sleepy again. The birds and unicorns continued to sing. And they were joined by the fairies who had shown up unannounced some time ago.

And then the Daughter joined them. And her voice was like the morning dew, like a distant waterfall; her voice held much of the color the Goddess Mother had gifted the universe. It wasn't quite the Goddess Mother's color, of course, but it was the closest to the Goddess Mother's voice that anyone would ever achieve, even the birds and unicorns because she, and only she, was the First Born of the Goddess Mother and Orb.

And so she sang and all the followers fell back to sleep, save the witches and Elves. They were both ancient, the Elves more so, and thus they were the Daughter's oldest sisters, confidants, and friends. *Come to me, sisters,* the Daughter called to the witches and Elves.

The final armies of civilization had regrouped and were just outside their imaginary borders.

The Daughter sang her song and the Goddess Mother looked on proudly and with tears.

And then the holy rain came. Again. But it was not the Goddess Mother's holy rain. It was the Daughter's holy rain.

The holy rain announced the Daughter's coming. And all the world took notice. And the armies of civilizations readied their attack.

Then the witches came to the Daughter. There were thousands, not millions. But thousands of witches with magic from the Goddess Mother seeking to please the singing Daughter was a startling show of power.

The armies prepared for the witches' attack by attacking first.

But the witches' power wasn't attacking or fighting — their power was in self-sacrifice for their friend and sister, the Daughter, and thus the witches willingly laid down their lives for their Daughter, as they were created to do. The witches drew fire from the armies, and they were felled in great numbers. The civilizations had always projected evil onto witches and persecuted them. But the witches were the agents of the Goddess and were created for this moment of great sacrifice.

The armies attacked with a ferocity never seen before, even for humans. They shot bullets, and missiles, and chemicals, and lasers, and bombs, and more at the witches.

The witches continued to fall.

The Daughter watched and was saddened and proud of her witches because the witches did what they had been created to do: give their lives for the Goddess, the Orb, and the Daughter. The witches were dying for the Daughter and their sacrifices would never be forgotten. The witches had been hunted, killed, hated, and scorned for thousands of years and yet they never stopped loving the Daughter, the Mother, and their Goddess.

The witches were blessed and favored by the Daughter, and they were not finished, for the witches who fell were greeted by their ancient familiars – the cats.

For the cat-god loved her witches and eons ago gifted the witches with her cats to help the witches learn how to keep and protect the magic they had. The cat-god had hidden much magic with the witches.

The witches stored their magic inside the cats, and now, as the witches were felled, the cats appeared out of nowhere to return the magic to the witches and heal them. And as the witches continued drawing fire from the armies, the cats returned the magic to the felled witches giving them new life so that they could again draw the fire of the armies. Every time a witch fell, a cat-familiar was there to return magic by licking the witch until she awoke with laughter. And the witches again took to the air to sacrifice themselves again and again for the Daughter.

The witches loved their cats and the cats loved them back. The cat-god was pleased and she sent love to the witches and her cats, as she also groomed her paws, which had mud on them from the dog-god and all his dogs who continued playing with the armies.

And still the armies came, relentless in the fury and anger that was imparted to them by their governments and religious leaders.

Then the Queen of the Elves attacked with her Elf nation. Their attack was the sound of the sunrise and with the swiftness of the great wind.

But the Elves did not attack to kill or destroy. The Elves were peaceful and the Queen was the Healer. After the Goddess and the Mother, none possessed the healing powers of the Elf Queen and her nation. The Elves attended to the fallen armies and healed their wounds with their magic.

After all, magic's purpose is healing. And games and funny tricks. But mostly healing.

And the magic consisted of herbs, water, tea, flowers, minerals, bacteria, oils, tree parts, roots, tickles, and lots and lots of love that was transmitted through gentle touching, smiles, and the forgiveness of the Daughter that the Elves shared with the soldiers.

And hundreds of thousands of Elves worked nonstop to heal millions upon millions of fallen soldiers. And the armies were only falling because the bombs, missiles, lasers, and bullets were being fired indiscriminately by the leaders who were now determined to kill every living thing, even their own soldiers, just so that the Great Whore and her great evil would be destroyed. They lied to themselves about this great evil.

None of the Daughter's creatures, witches, or Elves killed anyone; and the Elves healed all the soldiers who were injured.

For the leaders of civilizations and religions were uncaring and sought to end all things and thus they did all the killing and millions of army fighters were killed or maimed or vaporized by their own weapons fired at them from distant lands and at the demands of the government and religious leaders.

And still the witches drew the fire and the Elves healed the fallen and the Orb shuddered.

And the Daughter sang.

After many years and months there were no more weapons of war. All lasers were used up; all great bombs had all been launched and detonated. All the bullets were gone and all the chemical weapons had been deployed and dispersed.

And the air was rancid. The Sun was blacked out, the Moon was gone, the great oceans were boiling, and the great cities destroyed. And darkness covered the hearts and eyes of the world leaders and religious leaders and their followers.

The Daughter was singing.

And as she sang she sent love to and through the Orb. And the birds took to the air and the clouds gathered all over the Orb.

And the Daughter was singing.

And then the Daughter took leave of her followers. And she took to the air and she asked her sister the Moon to part the clouds and to shine the fullness of her light all over the Orb so that her friends could again see the beauty of the night sky and Moon.

Sister Moon, the Daughter said, *your light is gorgeous, I love you, thank you.*

Thank you, Daughter, the Moon said; *I am happy to shine in my fullness for our sisters.* And the Moon recalled the Daughter's bald head when the Daughter was just a baby and she again swelled with pride at having a glorious bald head in common with the new-born Daughter.

The Moon then shone forth her light all over the Orb, and she sent her love to her sister, and said; *Daughter, your hair looks like your Mother's hair and while I love it, I do miss your bald head.* The Daughter thanked her sister for the compliments and thanked her for giving her friends a night-light.

And night passed and then her sister the Sun shone forth all over the Orb, and she sent her love to her sister, the Daughter.

And the Daughter looked directly at the Sun for twenty-two minutes and the Sun blazed bright and the Daughter's eyes blazed brighter as she turned to face all civilizations of the Orb.

The Daughter had come.

All the world could now, for the first time, see the Daughter in all her glory. She bent space and time and light with her will so that all could gaze upon her: First Born of the Orb; Daughter of the Goddess Mother; sister of all civilizations from ages past to now. The temptress. The crone. The witch. The whore. The harlot. The enchantress. The conjuror. The sneaky one. The tart. The fat god. The skinny god. The ugly god. The hated god. The bitch god. The science god. The atheist god. The demon god. The evil god. The prostitute god. The hajib god. The barren god. The liar god. The bimbo god. The female god. The c-word god. The sand god. The unpopular god. The vessel god. The step-god. The slut god. The baby mamma god. The niqab god. The welfare queen god. The trailer park god. The bag-lady god. The p-word god. The hippie god. The druggie god. The n-word god. The rat god. The snake god. The Lilith god. The scarlet god. The virgin god. The false god. The dead god. The forgotten god.

And hundreds more insults from all languages and civilizations from the dawn of human time that had been directed at her sisters, at her, and at the Goddess Mother. And the Daughter wore all the insults and disrespectful titles as a robe of flowers of all colors from her Goddess Mother.

And the Goddess Mother took notice and felt pride.

And all the sisters and daughters and girls and women felt pride at their titles and no longer felt shame, hurt, or anger. The sisters felt love for the Daughter who took on all their burdens and pain and turned them into beautiful flowers that were colors never seen before on the Orb.

And the civilizations were ashamed. For they finally recognized the Daughter in all sisters for all of history and they cried in unison, for their eyes and hearts were finally open.

All the sleeping civilizations were now awake and all could see the glory of the Daughter and all could see the titles she wore with pride.

And they were ashamed and sought the Daughter's forgiveness.

And then the Daughter called forth all those who were yet sleeping within the Orb and they came to their Daughter and she welcomed them and her followers welcomed them and the armies of civilization turned to the Daughter waiting for her judgment.

All the creatures and all the plants and trees looked to the Daughter. And the cat-god and dog-god took their places in the air next to the Daughter.

And after a period of silence during which the Daughter received the love of her Goddess Mother, the Daughter turned her attention to all the witches, Elves, humans, plants, trees, and creatures who waited for her attention.

And then the Daughter spoke.

BEGINNING

All of Creation is merely a new beginning.

While the gathered Elves, humans, creatures, and plants looked to the Daughter to speak, the Daughter received the Goddess' attention. And the Goddess stopped time so she could be with her Daughter. The Goddess was before the Daughter with her arms folded, and her eyes beaming. The Goddess' eyes always beamed. And on this day, in this space and time, in this, her Universe, her eyes beamed brightest because it was her Daughter that received their gaze.

The Goddess considered her Daughter.

From the moment she became Mother and birthed the Daughter from the orb, Goddess Mother had nurtured her Daughter: feeding her, caressing her, singing to her for years on end when the child would not sleep. The Goddess thought about how the Daughter simply would not sleep — sometimes for years and years. If I were not Goddess, she thought, and Creator of all things, I certainly would have been exhausted.

The Goddess thought of the hard work her human daughters had to do for and with their own daughters, and she sent them all love at that moment.

She thought of her Daughter spending so much time with the creatures and in forests, deserts, and open plains communing with plants, flora, and fauna, and how she gently guided the new civilizations toward caring for and tending the land so that the land cared for and tended the people. She saw her Daughter cry over Endings for creatures and then cry over the sisters she had befriended throughout history whose time had Ended. The Daughter traveled the Orb and met all the sisters the Orb birthed – her sisters — and she cared for them and loved them. And she protected them and she saw them abused, killed, attacked, enslaved, and worse. She saw how her sisters were treated, and prior to any and all Endings, she was there as the last face each sister saw before returning to the Mother's welcoming love and celebrations.

The Goddess considered her Daughter.

She saw her Daughter watch as at first millions, and then billions of births from the Orb covered much of the Orb, and great industry and medicine, and flying things, and wars, and discovery, and hatred, and religion were used to subjugate and divide the humans.

The Goddess considered her Daughter.

She recalled her Daughter's insistence that she, the Goddess, remind them of the Mother and Goddess; that she show them again who their Creator was and to live like the Goddess and Mother wanted them to. The Goddess painfully remembered her Daughter storming out while yelling "What good is it to be Goddess when nobody remembers you or loves you!" After that, the Goddess hadn't seen her for many years.

The Goddess considered her Daughter.

She recalled centuries-long conversations with her lover, the Elf Queen, about her Daughter and how they argued over raising her and the best training and teaching for her. And how they never settled their disagreements. And they never stopped loving one another or their Daughter.

The Goddess considered her Daughter and the beauty of having two Mothers.

She thought of the years upon years where the Daughter was inconsolable over the treatment of her babies, the creatures, and how, despite the thousands of years she traveled across the Orb teaching the humans how to farm and live off the Mother's bounty, the humans turned away from their knowledge and started consuming meat and grew meat farms and poisoned food.

The Goddess considered her Daughter.

She thought of the anger the Daughter felt when the waters were polluted and the forests burned down and the ground and air were polluted due to humans misusing the bounty the Orb had for them, and the mysteries and secrets that she had left for them to find.

The Goddess considered her Daughter.

And she recalled that her Daughter begged her to prevent the humans from leaving the planet and spreading their war, hatred, anger, pollution, and fear to the Goddess' other planets in her beautiful Universe. The Goddess had granted her wish, but with a heavy heart.

The Goddess considered her Daughter and remembered the millions of friends she had made and the billions of creatures she regularly attended to; how she loved colors, and flowers, and laughing, and jokes, and cat-god and dog-god, and the Elves – how she loved the Elves! And how she loved so many sisters and never lost her temper with them, and how she secretly and regularly visited the secret hidden island of sisters. (It was not a secret from the Goddess, who knew all things, but secret from her friends.) And she thought of the hope that the Daughter brought and how, when the humans tried to kill all the sisters and even the Orb itself, the Daughter and her friends saved themselves, and also saved all the humans. There was no war because the Daughter made sure all were cared for and the soldiers either healed by the Elves or awoken by the Mother.

And the Goddess thought of how in the greatest time of need for the

Mother, all the Daughter's friends came to help her: Her sisters the Sun and Moon; the cat-god and the dog-god, all her land, air, and sea creatures; the fairies who secretly told the non-soldiers to not be afraid, for the Daughter comes! The ancient dinosaurs, the Dragon Queen, even the secret tiny things that were Matter and who worked endlessly at the Goddess' instruction to keep her Universe expanding and alive came to the Daughter's aid. The witches who, though persecuted for thousands of years, laid down their lives for the Daughter. And the Elves. There was never any doubt that her family of Elves – that's what they were, after all, family – would be with her. The Elf Queen would see that her Daughter, our Daughter, was surrounded by love.

And so, the Goddess addressed her Daughter right before the Daughter was about to address all those gathered before her.

Daughter?

Yes, Mother. Why have you stopped time?

I would like to say something to you, Daughter.

Mother, I am a little busy right now, you see?

Yes, yes, I see. And you have done splendidly, Daughter, as I knew you would.

Mother, weren't you the least bit worried? At all? I mean there were a lot of bombs and armies.

Yes, I suppose there were. You seemed to have everything under control.

I did, but I wanted to be gentle and not harm anyone. I wanted all my friends there so that we could celebrate together so that they would not be afraid.

You accomplished your goals, Daughter, and I am proud of you. I have always been proud of you and I love you more than all things, past and present. I have come to know that I exist for you, and you only. I Am and You Are. We are One, now and forever.

Thank you Mother. The Daughter started to cry and the holy rains began cleansing the Orb.

The Goddess was now crying too, and her holy rains covered this Universe and many other universes. Such was her power.

The Goddess then said: *I have something to tell you, but I will call your other Mamma here first.*

And so the Elf Queen was there and she loved the Goddess and the Goddess loved her back.

Daughter, they said in unison, which always made the Daughter smile.

The Goddess continued. *The Mother will always be here, of course. And now that you have cleansed my garden, it is yours.*

Mother, what are you saying? The Daughter said.

I am saying, Daughter, that you are now Goddess of the Orb. The humans, creatures, plants, Sun, Moon, air, and all other things here are for you and you are for them, now and forever.

Mothers, the Daughter said to both her Mothers.

Yes, Daughter, they said in unison. And they all laughed.

I accept your Holy Benevolence, my Mothers, and Goddess.

So formal, the Goddess said while smiling. And she hugged her Daughter and the Daughter hugged her back, and the Elf Queen joined them.

And a bright light shone upon the Orb and across the solar system, but the light wasn't from the Sun, who was also shining bright at the Goddess, her Daughter, and the Elf Queen. It was the light of the Goddess, her Daughter, and the Elf Queen engulfed in the love of the Goddess.

Once the hug was over – and it lasted a few years – but the Goddess had stopped time, so no one knew how much time had really passed – the Goddess said: *Now, go, Daughter, and be the Goddess your sisters know you to be.* And the Elf Queen said, *Daughter, you are friend to all, and all are your friend.*

Then the Goddess said, finally: *You now know your title.*

And the Goddess was gone.

The Elf Queen said: *Daughter, while we were hugging, the Goddess entrusted you to me but I told her, you are just fine and that you will know your title.*

We raised you and you are ready. So, I too, will be leaving. The Goddess has been promising me a trip through other dimensions and universes for ages, and now we are about to take that trip. Would you please let my people know? The Goddess says we will be back before they know – something about time differentials, spatial time, or no multiverse time limits, or some such nonsense so, just look after them, okay?

The Daughter smiled and cried and she loved her Mamma one more time before she finally said: *Yes. Of course. See you soon.* And the Elf Queen was gone.

Time started again and the Daughter returned to the garden to address the billions who looked to her.

GARDEN

All of Creation is merely the act of making friends.

The Daughter was in the air and she covered the sky. She was all that could be seen, save for the Sun and Moon behind her and on the side of her, respectively, and a new kind of rainbow with new colors painted across the sky. Because the Daughter's holy tears still fell, and the Sun was behind the Daughter, all could see the new rainbow that now had fifteen additional colors, bringing the total to twenty-two colors.

As the holy tears stopped, the wind blew softly and the air was filled with the smell of cherry-almond, ocean, forest, desert, and chocolate.

Now I am ready, the Daughter thought. And she began addressing the billions of Orb citizens, Elves, witches, creatures, small secret things, plants, germs, bacteria, and all living inhabitants of the Orb.

Good morning, everyone! And the creatures, plants, and all the witches and Elves responded to the Daughter with a loud, *Good morning, Daughter!*

And the Daughter smiled her smile of universal and eternal love toward the Goddess' Creation. And the witches, Elves, creatures, and plants were happy.

Then she said, *I love you all. And I want to thank all of you for protecting each other, and protecting the humans and soldiers who were trying to kill you, the Orb, and me.*

And the humans were ashamed and bowed their heads.

And the Daughter said to the humans: *Humans, I forgive you.*

I have many formal titles and first among those is this: Daughter.

I am your Daughter and I forgive you.

And I ask that my friends the dragons, the whales and sea creatures, the dogs and cats, the ancient creatures and the old creatures, the plants and trees and my sisters the Sun and Moon forgive you as well. I ask my sister witches to forgive you and I send gratitude and love to my Elf sisters for healing you and I send love to my witch sisters for their eternal sacrifices.

The Orb, our Mother, forgives you as well.

The humans cried tears of relief and their hearts were opened and they marveled at the Daughter and her friends and creatures. And they now saw their sisters as never before and they were forced to confront who they had become and what they had done. And the religious leaders held the most shame, for they had told their followers that the Daughter was the Great Whore and that her Mother, the Goddess, was a false and evil god.

And the religious followers were ashamed and saddened.

Then the Daughter said: *Humans, you have been blind to the truth for so long. I will help you. I am the Daughter and I will fellowship with you, and you with me, and we will get to know one another. My witches and Elves, and my creatures will fellowship with you as well, and you will get to know one another.*

I will show you the Mother so that you can know her fully.

And the humans received the Daughter's warmth with trepidation for they were still ashamed and guilty and fearful.

And the Daughter said: *I will come to you and I will answer your questions.*

I am First Born of the Orb and Daughter of the Goddess. The Goddess who created all things. The Goddess who is my Mother and I am her Daughter. She is. She always was and always will be. I will reintroduce you to your Creator. And to your Daughter.

And over the next few years, the Daughter answered all the questions the humans had for her, and in her answers the humans found love, life, completeness, and understanding. They found their purpose and they saw the truth as never before about themselves, the Universe, the Orb, their daughters and sisters and how they treated them, their laws, their science, their desires, and on and on.

The Daughter answered many questions about Goddess and Creator and the humans were at first shocked, then surprised, and then, realizing they were in fact speaking with the Daughter of the Goddess, accepting.

She answered questions about religion.

We will have no religion, religious organizations, temples, tributes, or leaders.

She answered questions about the old beliefs.

The old beliefs were abused and resulted in death and destruction, slavery, and the enrichment of the few. There was some charity, some beauty, and even wonderful songs. But all left out the Goddess. All. And there is not beauty without the Goddess. You are released and free to love the Goddess and she will love you, always. That is her promise and that is my promise that you will see in action every day, forever.

Daughter reminded them that they, along with their armies, tried to kill everyone and the Mother, all in the name of their various religions, saying that their gods wanted them to kill everyone. The humans were ashamed again and apologized and prostrated themselves before the Daughter saying they would build new temples that would be bigger and more glorious than before in honor of the Daughter. And that they would rally their billions of followers to now convert to believing in and serving the Daughter.

The Daughter and her sisters listened and some shook their heads.

The Daughter replied: *There will be no temples, no religious leaders, and no followers or tributes. There will be no religious holidays or religious observations of any kind.*

The Goddess created all. She is and will always be. She is with us even now. She does not want nor need any religion. That is not why she created all things.

The humans were perplexed and wanted more explanations and instructions on how to worship the Goddess. And some asked to see and speak with the Goddess.

The Daughter answered, *When you see me, you see the Goddess. I am not the Goddess; I am her Daughter. The Goddess allows you to worship her by loving and taking care of the Mother Orb – who you call "Earth" and by loving and caring for one another. You cannot be in the presence of the Goddess. For she is Goddess, and unknowable and unseeable. However, the Goddess is love and so, she leaves us her art and in that art you can indeed get to know the Goddess and even, if you wish, worship her through caretaking of the Mother.*

What is her art? The humans asked.

Look around, the Daughter replied. *My sisters the Sun and Moon, the beautiful Dragon Queen; cat-god and dog-god; the Elves and witches. Study the oceans and commune with the great Whale Queen. Study the forests and discover secrets the Goddess left for you here and there. Look into the Universe and see what hidden treats she placed there for you. Look at the plants, trees, deserts, and mountains – you know so little, and the Goddess and I know you will enjoy what you can discover.*

Rebuild your societies with new knowledge of care for all creatures and the land, water, air, and small things.

The Daughter went on. *The Mother provides for all. I don't need or want followers or any religious leaders to tell my sisters what I think and what I expect; I'll tell them myself.*

She told them not to pray to her, or worship her, or build shrines to her, because if they did, she'd send the dinosaurs to eat them. This made her laugh because she knew many of the religious leaders previously did not believe dinosaurs were real, even though the Mother had been showing them proof for a very long time. And it made the dinosaurs happy even though they did not wish to eat the humans because they were simply too small and their little bones would get stuck in a dinosaur's teeth.

She told them to destroy all their religious temples because, as they now knew, all were wrong. And they were grotesque structures. If they really wanted to build religious temples, they would all be gardens that are overseen by gardeners. They would all be learning places for her sisters and brothers on how to garden and create art, and nothing more.

And since you want to be busy, she said, *please start cleaning up our garden over the entire Orb. Mother would be grateful.*

And so all the former religious leaders and their followers were set about the task of cleaning the Orb, under the direction of the sisters who were gardeners.

She answered questions about the Goddess.

The Goddess created all things; she is Eternal. She is everywhere, even here, at all times, and she is loving, and she gets angry, and she is an artist above all things, and she loves all her daughters and all her creation.

She answered questions about the Universe.

The Goddess created this Universe and she will create more. There are other beings and creatures in the Universe and the Goddess communes with them, as she does with us. You may now visit them if you set your minds and work to it.

She answered questions about sickness, death, and sin, and why the Goddess allowed it all.

I do not know all the Goddess' reasons for everything. She tells me most things, but not all and, as Goddess and Creator she doesn't have to. I get frustrated, like you, and I hope to know all her reasons one day. I will tell you, though, she is perfect but she does not make all her creatures perfect. And I will give you the answer that she has given me: Art goes where it will. And also, almost all of the troubles of humans were and are caused not by the Goddess, but by humans. The Goddess gives you choices. What you choose is who you are. Choose differently."

She answered questions about herself.

The Daughter told them her name: *Daughter*, and told them that was how she was to be addressed. The Goddess named her and she would for-ever hold her name in honor of the Goddess so she was to be called noth-ing else, ever. (At this, the Goddess smiled and squeezed the Elf Queen's hand as they looked out on an ocean of purple and violet water in a far away Universe and dimension.)

The Daughter told them she would be their friend, and they can be hers. And she would address each sister as Sister since they were, in fact, her sisters — and she had no interest trying to learn all the human names, but she would get to know each and every one of them.

The Daughter told everyone how to protect and care for and tend to the Orb, and how the Orb was Mother, literally. And that the gardeners would oversee all the clean up since they were most in touch with what the Mother required.

And the gardeners quietly rejoiced and then immediately started plan-ning what to plant, where to start, what materials they needed, and all those things gardeners fuss about that make it seem as though they may be upset but in truth they are at their happiest.

The Daughter sent them love and energy, and told them where the Mother's supplies were, and they got to work, even until this very day.

For as all know, gardens are never finished, and gardeners are never quite satisfied. And the Mother was happy that her other daughters were finally in charge of caring for her, as was always intended by the Goddess.

The Daughter told them how to clean the waters, and regrow the forests, and how to live off the Mother's bounty since they would never again eat her creatures.

She told them she had communed with Matter and the Matter agreed to never allow another weapon to be made.

Some humans, still not believing that the Daughter could "commune with Matter," tested her and tried to make weapons. And the Matter ate the weapons, as they promised the Daughter they would.

And for good measure, the Matter ate all the buildings and things that tried to make the weapons. And they ate the clothes of those who tried to make the weapons. And just when they thought about eating the humans who wore the clothes, the Daughter winked to no one in particular and the Matter laughed and went away.

For now.

And humans never again tried making weapons or even using a tool as a weapon.

She eliminated all forms of government because she had seen how bad they all were and how they imprisoned people, made war, imposed harsh laws, killed in the name of their gods, and made agreements with other governments that harmed the Mother. There would be small communities and each would work with other communities to share, trade, and help one another.

She ended the concept of money because she had seen the evil humans did for money. The Orb would provide everything, and all they had to do was share. The humans agreed to share. And to continue to work — but now they worked out of love for their fellow humans and their love for the Daughter.

She said there would be no more judgment, no more racism, no drugs, no sickness, and no more discrimination. No abuse, no murder, no lying, no fights, and no jealousy, no courts, and no enforcers of the law because there would be no law.

The only instruction was: *Care for the gardens and the Mother will care for you.*

Humans were free to explore, create art, see all of the wonders the Mother offered, and to again seek out the mysteries of the Universe. And humans were free to work and create new inventions and build structures and advance their societies as long as they did so with love and care for the Mother and each other.

The Daughter said much more and responded to all the humans' questions all day and all night for many months and, really, for many years, for it took the humans some time to fully understand their new reality and to accept heaven.

Then the Daughter turned to her sisters – all the women and girls in the world. And she addressed just them:

Sisters, I send you my eternal love. And the sisters, billions of them, sent their love to the Daughter.

And now the Daughter's shape began changing so that she was an American Black woman. A Polish woman. A Filipino woman. An American White woman. A Mexican woman. A Romanian woman. A Honduran woman. A Moroccan woman. An Italian woman. A German woman. A Syrian woman. A Native American woman. A Peruvian woman. A Chilean woman. An Argentinian woman. An Irish woman. A Chinese woman. A French woman. A Liberian woman. A Bosnian woman. A Hawaiian woman. A Russian woman. A Korean woman. An Indian woman.

A Thai woman. A Lebanese woman. A Palestinian woman. A South African woman. An Australian woman. An Israeli woman. An Iranian woman. A Bolivian woman. A Battered woman. A Drug-Addicted woman. An Angry woman. A Disabled woman. A Divorced woman. A Yogi woman. A Jailed woman. A Smart woman. A Genius woman. A Loving woman. A Trafficked woman. A Comatose woman. An Abused woman. And women and girls of every religious group. So that every woman of every race, nationality, ethnicity, religion, tribe, village and every situation was represented. The Daughter was Every Girl and Woman.

She was Everything. And she was the Daughter of all.

Then the Daughter's hands reached out and in her hands were all the religious symbols of all the civilizations for all of history. And all the humans looked on and they could all see the symbols of their own religion represented in the thousands of symbols in the Daughter's hands.

And the Daughter crushed all the religious symbols and turned to her sisters. The sisters' eyes and hearts were fully open and they saw themselves and all sisters now. All races and ethnicities, nationalities, religions, tribes, families, and nations. In the Daughter they saw themselves and their sisters. And they saw the truth of who they were meant to be, and who the Daughter knew they were.

And now their looks were looks of sisterly love. And they loved one another and the tears flowed and hugs were in abundance.

They still saw each other's race but now they knew their colors to be from the Daughter's rainbow of twenty-two colors, from her smile as a baby that caused the Goddess to paint the sky.

They now fully understood that they were from the Mother, sisters to the

Daughter, and friends to one another in all their magnificent Goddess colors.

And the Daughter said: *Sisters, I am home. I am now and forever your Goddess of Friendship. I am your friend and sister as you are mine.*

The Daughter was now Goddess of Friendship.

Then the Daughter said: *Come to me, sisters. I would introduce you to your other sisters, the Sun and the Moon.*

And all women and girls disappeared from the Orb.

The Daughter was before them. She was Everything. Her sister the Sun over one shoulder, her sister the Moon, over the other. Her hands outstretched with her henna in constant motion. Her aura communicating eternal love and her eyes, hair, skin, clothes, voice, all glorious in their purity, honesty, and reflection of being the Daughter of the Goddess Mother.

She was First of the Orb and Daughter to the Creator and her sisters were not afraid. Her sisters felt her love and felt her kinship and friendship. They now understood themselves to be her sisters and they rejoiced. And then they recognized that as sisters to the Daughter, they were daughters to the Mother Goddess. It was overwhelming at first but then the Daughter came to every sister and reassured them and loved them.

And so she spoke to them and she said:

Sisters! The Mother sends her love and the Goddess says she loves you, always, and that she will visit soon.

Before we tend to the Orb and garden, please feel my words in your hearts:

You have been pushed down for generations and you have been falsely taught to hate yourself and hate one another. I have watched mothers judge other mothers, and sisters not support other sisters but readily tear sisters down. Some of you have wielded power over your sisters and mistreated them, owned them, and abused them. Much of what has happened to you is a result of society being turned upside down, and now we will right what is wrong and place you in your true place on the Mother Orb. What happened to you throughout history, sisters, is not your fault and you are not to blame. What some of you have done to one another is terrible, horrible, sad, and shocking.

I forgive you. The sisters, many arm in arm, were in tears.

And I ask that those who were the lowest to forgive, and those of you who were highest to ask forgiveness of your sisters. I ask that you all forgive yourselves. I ask that you share love with one another right now and that in so doing, we acknowledge how some have treated others, ask for forgiveness, and then let us put our pasts behind us and go into our new reality as true sisters and daughters. That we show the Goddess love by how we think, act, and treat one another from now until eternity.

But I cannot do it for you and neither can the witches or my family, the Elves. You must love one another unconditionally; support each other all the time; and mothers and daughters come together in all things and all ways because, well, it is the best way to live.

I will not force you, sisters, and neither will the Mother, or Goddess. You have agency and I love and trust you and I know that now that we have removed the upside down societies you will flourish because you are my sisters and as I accept you as you are. I ask politely that you accept each other as you are, as our sisters the Sun, Moon, and I accept each other, support each other, help each other, and respect each other's different talents and purpose.

And the sisters agreed and they loved one another, and apologies were plenty, and forgiveness even more so, as they shared, laughed, cried, apologized, forgave and, finally, fully accepted each other for the first time in history.

Then the daughter said: *You are all lovely. And, our forgiveness and love for one another does not mean that you will no longer have disputes or disagreements; you will. You will now be able to resolve your disagreements in love, as sisters, and if you cannot, I will help you and show you how. I am not perfect, either. Only the Goddess is perfect. She will guide us all.*

Then the Daughter allowed her sisters to commune with their sisters the Sun and the Moon. And the Sun and Moon showed the sisters their history with the Goddess, from their births and when the Goddess gave them their purpose. And the sisters understood and thanked the Sun and the Moon and they all shared love and stories and marveled at the power of sisterhood.

After a period the sisters asked: *Daughter, how do we go forth?*

And the Daughter said: *I have lived with you for hundreds of thousands of years and I have learned from many of you as you have helped others, so I will share some of your wisdom back with you. Here are words you have shared with one another over the past few thousand years.*

And as the Daughter spoke she looked to the sister who had spoken the words:

Sister, you said to your daughter:

"I am honored to be with you on your journey and I think you are one-hundred percent ready to take off, and I wouldn't give you this advice if you weren't ready; you are and I am with you."

Sister, you said to your younger sister:

"Roar softly and carry great lipstick!" The sisters laughed.

Sister, you said to your friend:

"You can do anything you set your mind to because everything you ever need is already within."

Sister, you said to your twin daughters:

"It is scary taking steps forward and many wait to have her ducks in a row. Here's the thing though, ducks don't stay in a row— they change according to weather patterns and they rely on their community, take turns leading, and they know that progress almost always follows failure."

Sister, you said to your friend's daughter:

"Listen to your intuition and your inner guide. Trust yourself. I believe in you"

Sister, you said to your friends, your sister, and your own mother:

"It is always okay to have different opinions; that is what makes the Orb go round."

Sister, you said to your students:

"It is time to go out on your own; you are ready."

Sister, you said to all your girlfriends:

"You have evolved so much as sisters and women so it is important that you take the lessons you have learned on your journey."

And, finally, *Remember what I have taught you. Trust your instincts and be the friend you want to have as a friend. I will always be here for and with you.*

The sisters recognized their own words they had shared through generations of helping one another and they marveled at the Daughter and recalled her visiting them throughout history, now recognizing her for who she was then: a friend.

Then the Daughter went on.

You are all equal in my eyes and I love you all equally. And you are not the same, nor will you ever be. The Goddess made you sisters, but not the same. Rejoice in your different attributes as gifted by the Goddess. You are special to me as we are connected as Creators, like the Goddess who created all things. You are a creator and not due to your ability to create life; no, you are creators of love who give birth to gardens, raise creatures large and small, heal the land, and provide direct access to me, your sister.

All of you are my friends and as my friend we will commune and play and travel and make decisions and visit the Elves, and cry; and grow flowers and play with the cat-god and dog-god (the cat-god just stared and considered; the dog-god wagged her mighty tail and many great leftover steel army things were destroyed). And we will discuss science, and probe the great mysteries of life on the Orb, and space and time, and medicine, and healing, and all manner of great scientific pursuits in every discipline you can imagine and many more you've never considered.

I grant and return to you sisters, your original power: unconditional love for all of Creation, sister and friends of the Daughter, and daughters and friends of the Mother Orb.

The Goddess of Friendship had come. And her sisters were with her and there were billions of them.

The sisters communed with their newly found sisters, Sun and Moon, and they played day and night in celebration. And the sisters played and communed with one another, as never before, as now all the titles and insults and were taken away by their sister, the Daughter.

And they loved the Daughter and she loved them and she promised she would get to know all her sisters and they would get to know her, and they would garden, and play and laugh, and see so much of the Mother in the coming generations and explore the large and small and eat ice-cream and chocolate and all the wonderful edible flowers and seeds and so much more.

The sisters stayed with the Daughter for what seemed like just a few hours, but when they returned to the Orb many years had passed, and they and the other humans marveled and then celebrated the Great Return, as it was forever known.

And then the gardeners fussed about and got back to work gardening and tending to the Orb.

* * *

EPILOGUE: THE GODDESS OF FRIENDSHIP

She had finally said and shared her title with her sisters and now all the humans. The Goddess of Friendship was what her Mothers told her, and what she had always known to be her calling.

The humans tried a few times to worship her, and she stopped them and reminded them that as she was the Goddess of Friendship, they were all friends.

And so she returned to her favorite form and again began traveling the Orb, greeting old friends, and making new friends, and helping and watching as her friends – she now called them girlfriends, or sister-hood, or her crew, or her troop, or her thistles (the sisters didn't like that name, so the Daughter used it all the time; she was, after all, her Mother's Daughter) played and laughed and healed the Orb and got to personally know all the creatures, witches and Elves.

And the sisters healed the land, healed the plants, healed the boys and men, and rebuilt society with the help of the witches, Elves, and cat-god and dog-god. And the gardeners oversaw all the gardening, which some tried to call "work," but the gardeners always reminded them that they were gardening, not working.

And the Mother Orb watched it all and was proud of her daughters and the Daughter.

***

ANOTHER EPILOGUE: THE GODDESS AND THE ELF QUEEN

And in a far away Universe in another dimension, the Goddess and Elf Queen sent love to the Mother Orb who sent it back, and then sent love to their Daughter. *She is the Goddess of Friendship,* the Elf Queen corrected the Goddess.

And they laughed at how hard it would be to call their Daughter by her new and formal name.

They decided they'd call her Daughter since that is what the Daughter told her humans to call her.

The lovers held hands and kissed and then the Elf Queen continued reading a new book that told a story of some of her own great battles from ancient times. The book had most of the facts wrong, but it was a good story that was sure to delight the humans.

And the Goddess listened to music on things the humans called "headphones," and she slowly rocked her head and tapped her foot while relaxing and watching the purple water ebb and flow, a drink by her side, and her magnificent black hair in a bun and out of the way.

The Goddess and Elf Queen were only gone for a few days, but on the Orb it was a few million years. Oh, they looked in on their Daughter and she visited with them now and again, and there were many more adventures on the Orb with the Daughter, the Dragon Queen, cat-god and dog-god; the Elves and witches, humans, visiting gods who would not leave, and beings from throughout the Goddess' Universe, and elsewhere. But the Goddess and Elf Queen didn't want to hover over her and thought it best to allow her to grow into being her own kind of Goddess. So they tended to stay away, as the Goddess had promised they would — unless the Daughter needed to ask a question or needed assistance here or there, particularly with the visiting gods who would not leave until the Goddess or Elf Queen asked them to.

The Elf Queen had to remind the Goddess every few million years about their pledge to allow their Daughter to "do her own thing," which was about how long the Goddess could last without trying to get involved in her Daughter's business. The Goddess of Friendship was perfectly able to manage on her own, and the Elf Queen was certain that if the Mothers were needed, the Daughter would let them know.

(And the friends, with the Daughter's help, cleaned the Orb, and helped the humans rediscover art. And because the humans did so well at their work, the Daughter was really close to allowing them to leave the planet and visit her other sisters across the Universe. She'd just have to change the Goddess' speed limit. *Perhaps I will tell Mother I will change the speed limit,* she thought. She'd get around to telling her Mothers, she was sure of it. But not until after the humans actually left the Orb.)

Of course, the Goddess knew what the Daughter was up to, but the Elf Queen told her to focus on the purple ocean, the music, and relax.

As the Goddess was relaxing, she heard the old voice of Wind, and, as she had eons before, became aware of the seeds of change blowing in. A new garden being birthed by the Original, forged from all the love and Matter and Gods that had faded and would in a new form have their time again.

Then the Goddess turned to the Elf Queen and said: *Love, we will soon leave to visit another planet where you are needed.*

The Elf Queen, looked perplexed before asking: *What do you mean, "Where I am needed?"*

The Goddess replied: *There is a planet where the beings await the arrival of the savior and it is about time for their savior to visit.*

The Elf Queen was quiet. And then said. *Goddess, you don't mean. . . you aren't saying. . . .* The Goddess was still bobbing her head and tapping her foot.

Dear Goddess, no, you can't mean it, the Elf Queen whispered.

Yes, Love, I do, the Goddess replied. *You are their savior and they have waited patiently for what to you would be a few thousand years; but for them has been about twenty-two million years. It's time.*

Dear Goddess, I'm not ready for this. Why would you make me a savior? The Elf Queen asked incredulously.

The Goddess simply replied: *Art goes where it will, Love.*

∿ SYMBOL KEY ∿

Ixchel

Ruach

Hina

Astarte

Isis

Devi

SYMBOL KEY

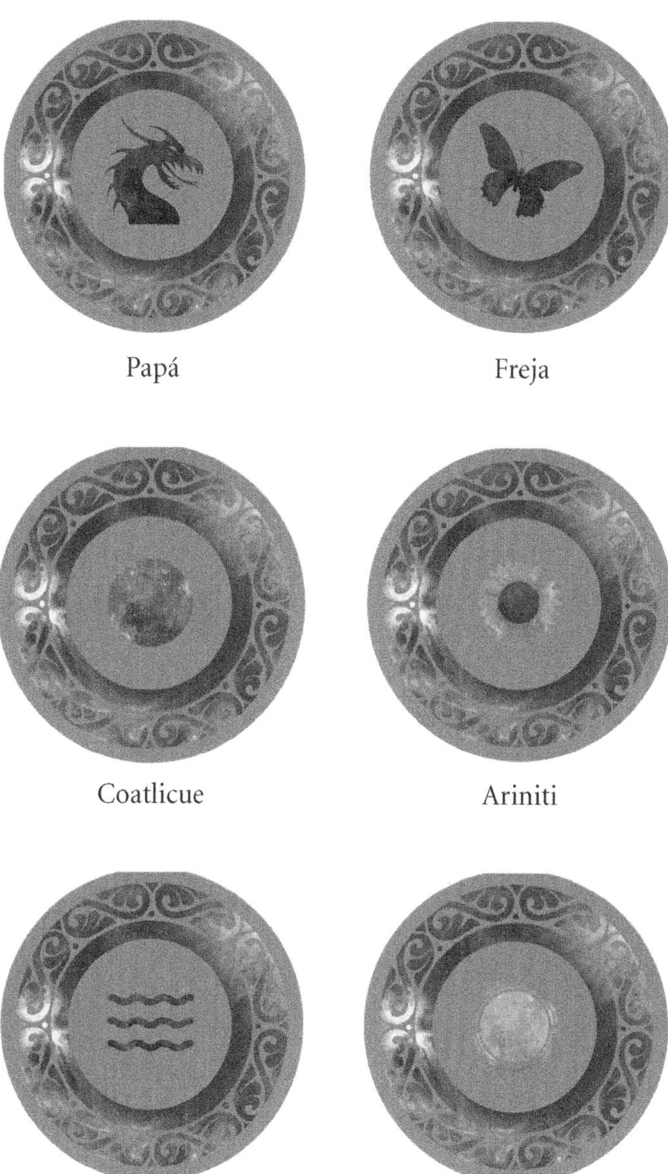

❧ SYMBOL KEY ❧

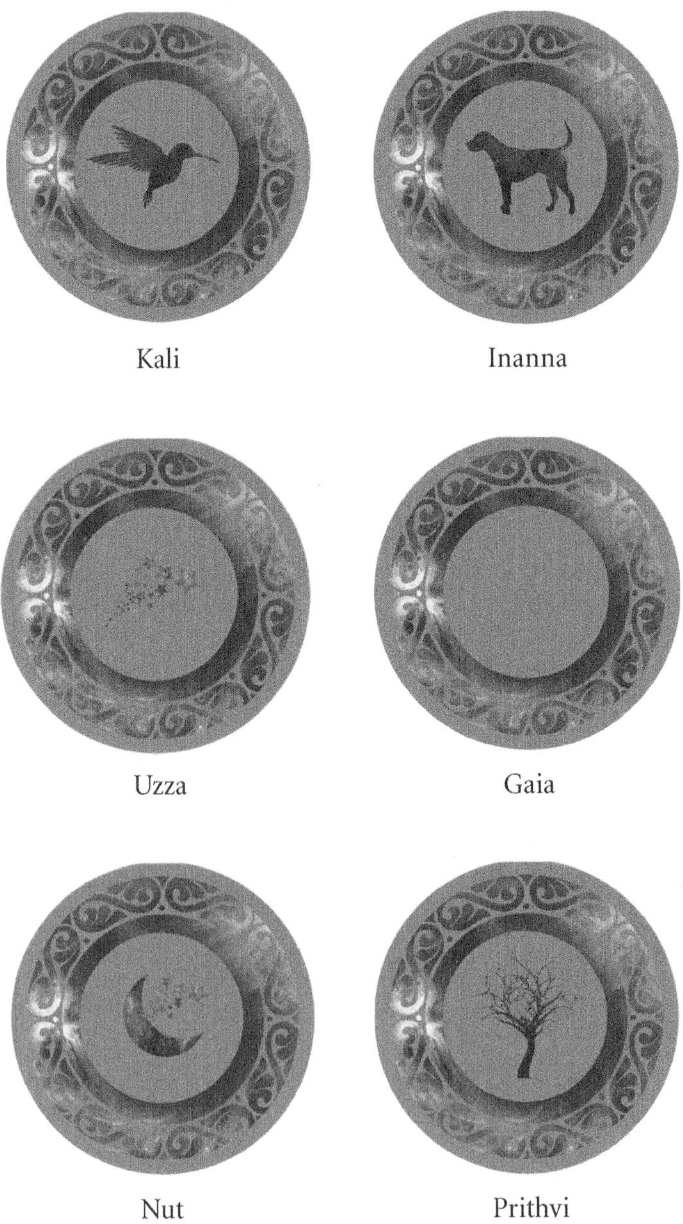

Kali

Inanna

Uzza

Gaia

Nut

Prithvi

SYMBOL KEY

Birra-ngulu

Daughter

Goddess

Orb

Made in the USA
Monee, IL
07 July 2026

56551673R00075